Clean Slate

Barbara Winkes

Chapter 1

"Are you sure about this, Rae?" Mark Castillo, her former partner and soon to be boss, asked, as they walked along the hallway.

Rachel Burton, Rae to her family and friends, gave the question some thought. If she felt a flutter in her stomach, it was from excitement—or nerves. Time would tell, and tell in a matter of hours, as tomorrow would be the first day with his unit.

As a detective, the way she wanted it. Some might think she was going backwards, but to Rae, it was an opportunity that wouldn't come back anytime soon. It was the path forward she needed.

"Can't wait."

"Good. I'm thrilled to have you on board. We have a good team here. You'll fit right in, and your experience is most welcome."

She almost winced, but his flattery was genuine, not a hint at the fact that she might be older than most of her colleagues, or that her experience meant she could be doing something else. Like staying in the office that she had occupied for the last two years. Rae had grown tired of that office and everything it represented, which only partly had to do with the job.

She was ready for a change, at least where her career was concerned. And it was up to her to decide what was best for her, now that she only had to take herself into consideration.

"Let me show you something," Mark said as he opened a door.

It led them to the observation area of the interrogation room. A detective and an A.D.A. watched as one of their colleagues was questioning a suspect. They acknowledged Mark and Rae with a nod and turned back to the glass.

Behind it, a man sat slumped in a chair, giving the other occupant of the room a patronizing grin.

The cop interrogating him was a woman, wearing a crisp business suit, her brown hair in a ponytail. She was pretty, Rae noticed, not that it was of any importance. She was asking all the right questions, and soon the suspect was sitting up straighter, his expression a lot less cocky than it had been a moment ago.

"Don't bother. We have proof. DNA puts you at the scene, and we have multiple witnesses. And the cameras you destroyed? Well, you forgot one."

Her voice was warm and pleasant, her tone light as if she was making small talk.

Rae could see the smile on Mark's face.

"They never see her coming," he said. "Dakota Lord. She's about to wrap this up, but there's another case she could use some help with, and you'd be perfect."

"Hm. If you say so."

"Rae."

"I assume there's no particular reason why you decided to partner me with the only other woman in your unit?"

"You're not serious." He sounded genuinely disappointed that she could think such a thing. "She has good instincts, but she could use a bit of guidance. Like I said, you'll be perfect."

"Thanks...and sorry about that."

"You're forgiven. How about a coffee before you go, and I tell you a little more about that case?"

Rae cast another look at Dakota who was perching on the edge of the table now. She was intrigued and a bit apprehensive at the same time. Once upon a time, she had been that rising star in her unit, determined to pursue a flawless career without any detours. That was before she realized how many variables in her life were truly out of her control.

But she was a team player, and she wanted to be on this team. Mark didn't hire her just to do her a favor.

It would be fine.

"Perfect. I'm curious."

She was curious about Dakota too, but she would have to wait until the next day.

The moment came quickly. After a sleepless night, excessive coffee consumption and the short drive to the station, Rae felt all eyes on her as Mark introduced her to the team, or at least, the detectives present.

"Everyone, this is Detective Rachel Burton. Detectives Nathan Baker and Dakota Lord. As most of you all know, Rae was my partner for five years. If she asks, I've only told you good things about her. Which is the truth," he said, earning some laughter from the small group.

Dakota Lord, wearing jeans and a black button-down shirt today, was the exception. She studied Rae with interest, more pensive than amused. Rae found it a bit unnerving, but she wasn't going to let that reaction deter her. If Lord was as good as Mark said, she'd be all about getting the work done. Rae was fine with that.

"Okay, you can go back to work. Rae? Detective Lord? I'd like to see you in my office."

"What did I do, boss?" Lord asked, the corners of her mouth twitching into a smile.

"The fact that you ask worries me. Come on."

Castillo didn't lose any time once they were behind closed doors.

"So, where are we?" He didn't need to go into any details.

He had filled Rae in the day before, and from what she knew, Detective Lord had been on the case from the beginning. A week ago, they had been called to a strange and disturbing scene. A thirty-four-year-old woman was dead in her own basement. The autopsy and tox screen had helped them rule out suicide after rat poison was found in her system.

"This wasn't an accident." Lord was leaning against the door, arms crossed over her chest. "There were no rats or poison anywhere in this house. We asked the neighbors. Sarah Cooper never mentioned any problems. Someone made her ingest a cocktail of sleeping pills with the poison."

"Any signs of that someone?"

"They were careful. Nothing yet from the lab. She lived alone, never saw anyone, according to the neighbors."

"This isn't good," he said with a frown.

Detective Lord didn't disagree, though her expression revealed she wasn't pleased.

"You spoke to the family? Boyfriend—or girlfriend?"

"Her mother and stepfather live in Oregon. They came over for the funeral. Cooper was single." The other detective cast her a quick curious look before she made the connection why Rae was here.

"Boss, no, I know what I'm doing."

"I'm aware. I still want Detective Burton on this case with you. She's cracked a few weird ones, and I'm sure you'll work well together."

"But..."

"I'm not asking," he warned. "I've told her the basics, you make sure she's up to date on any recent development. Now go back to work. Rae, your desk is across from Lord's."

"Thank you," she said, hurrying to follow the younger woman out of the office and to her assigned desk.

Dakota Lord took a folder from hers and put it in front of Rae.

"This is everything we have so far. Happy reading."

"Wait," Rae called after her when she walked away. "Where are you going?"

She cringed before the woman turned, irritation visible in her attractive features.

"I need a coffee."

She kept walking, and Rae decided to let it go for the moment. She wasn't here to make friends or enemies, though she found her reaction a bit over the top. Of course, Rae herself hadn't always accepted help when a supervisor decided it was for the best. She couldn't suppress the wry smile at a memory or two that came with the thought. All right. She was going to focus on what was right in front of her.

She started reading, quickly finding everything she was looking for. The case wasn't far advanced, as she had learned, but Rae was glad to find that the detective was thorough. Neighbors, friends, and family had been contacted and interviewed. Dakota had talked to her colleagues at the university. The picture of Sarah Cooper remained startlingly vague.

Rae paused over the statement of a friend who described Sarah as quiet. Still waters. Her mother had remarried after an abusive relationship. Rae aborted her impromptu theory when she found a note that Sarah's birth father had been dead for five years. She had rented the house a year ago. No one knew if she had dated anyone, though Rae assumed that she might not have been the type to share.

A mix of sleeping pills and rat poison...It almost looked like someone wanted them to know she was murdered, though not right away, throw them for a loop. Or someone had a specific picture in mind.

She looked up to see Dakota standing in front of her, carrying two paper cups with steaming coffee in them.

"I didn't know if you liked milk or sugar, so I brought both. Look—I didn't mean to start out on the wrong foot, but I know I can crack this case."

"I don't doubt that. Thank you." She'd had more than her share of caffeine already, but it might not be wise to refuse the peace offering. "I'm here to help."

"I don't need help, I need a fucking miracle," Dakota grumbled as she settled back behind her desk.

Rae pondered her choice of words for a few heartbeats. It wasn't like her own generation never used any expletives, though she thought they did it more sparsely and perhaps, in a different context. Irrelevant.

"You thought of everything."

"Thanks, I guess."

"Neighbor says she had a cat. You ever found it?"

"No." Dakota shook her head. "We searched the house top to bottom, no sign of it other than the litter box and a few photos on her mantel. It must have run away. What?" she asked, a smile appearing on her face. "You think it saw something? Brilliant idea. Find the cat, find the murderer."

"We should be so lucky," Rae mumbled, ignoring the jibe.

"Sorry. This is already bizarre. Rat poison, what is this, an Agatha Christie murder mystery?"

"It's a mystery all right. You spoke to Sarah's colleagues at the university. No weird vibes, anyone who might be jealous of her, someone she angered?"

"She was doing a lot of fundraising, and according to her co-workers, she was very good at it." Dakota pushed a strand of hair behind her ear, impatient. Rae couldn't help finding the gesture adorable even though she wasn't sure yet what to make of her attitude. There seemed to be something beyond the fact that she was used to working alone.

That begged the question, what exactly had Mark told his unit about her?

"That potentially involves a lot of money, doesn't it?"

"Yeah, sure, but why kill someone that way? If there was any dark money involved, believe me, those people don't need to go to those lengths. They know we can't trace them. The poison is still throwing me off."

"That is easy to get, the sleeping pills, they weren't over-the-counter. Her prescription?"

"I didn't find it in her papers...damn it."

She obviously realized that she might have overlooked something.

Rae sipped her coffee, not feeling triumphant. This might be just another detour...or dead end.

"Her papers were in immaculate order," Dakota said. "No prescription."

"I'd like to see the scene. And maybe drive by the university again. I'd like to get a better idea of what she was doing in her job, whom she was seeing."

"Knock yourself out." She caught herself in time. "I'm not sure what else we can find there, but I'm coming with you."

"Yes, of course. You mind if I drive?"

"No, not at all."

Despite the somewhat rocky start, Rae felt assured in her decision when they were en route to the university. Solving the puzzle, it was something she was good at. Being out in the field was far from how she had spent the past couple of years, juggling the demands of politics and inter-departmental diplomacy, and the needs of members of her unit who were out there doing the work.

They had told her they would miss her. She missed them too, but she still felt she could do more, and leave the job to someone who was less hands-on, and a more skilled communicator. Politician. Whatever.

She couldn't help being excited, though she was aware of Dakota Lord tapping her fingers on her jean-clad leg. She wasn't used to being in the passenger seat.

There were many interpretations for this, and she didn't have time for either of them.

They had arrived at the university where Sarah had her office in the administrative wing. Despite the dire occasion, Rae couldn't help admiring the architecture of one of the oldest buildings in the city. They housed a lot of knowledge and tradition...and tug of war, she assumed, when it came to funding. She knew that they regularly had big fundraising events. Several public figures, many of them alumni, were involved.

And then there was Sarah, the quiet efficient employee who had convinced many to open their wallets.

"The dean will see us for a few minutes," Dakota said. "You better have your questions ready."

The challenge in her tone was unmistakable.
"Don't worry," Rae returned. "I will."

Chapter 2

Dakota Lord couldn't believe her bad luck. She'd been on a brilliant trajectory in the past year, until this case. It had her stumped. It was dragging. It was the worst possible moment for Castillo to assign her a babysitter.

She frowned at her thought, knowing it was petty. She couldn't help herself. Of course, she had heard about Rae Burton. Mark wouldn't shut up about her whenever prompted.

Once upon a time, Dakota had considered her someone to look up to, from afar, but these days, irritation got the better of her. She didn't want to be that kind of person. Then again, she hadn't imagined Burton would be the kind of person who quit.

She might be experienced, the boss's friend, and undeniably gorgeous…She was not going to let her swoop in with a few good ideas and then take the credit, when Dakota had worked her behind off, on this case, and before.

She remained reasonably polite as she introduced her to Dean Lowell. "This is Detective Rachel Burton. She's going to work with me on Sarah's case." She almost said "assist", but she didn't want any more scrutiny, from Castillo or anyone else.

"Nice to meet you, Detective."

Still, Dakota couldn't help frowning when Rachel launched into the same line of questioning she had already been through with the dean, and gotten nowhere. She could observe though that Rachel put the woman at ease. She and Lowell were approximately the same age.

People still guessed Dakota to be younger, thus less experienced, than she was. She pushed the thought aside and listened, studying the dean's demeanor as she answered Rachel's questions.

"You told my colleague that Sarah never had any problems with co-workers. What about the donors? Did anyone ever mention dissatisfaction with her work?"

The dean shook her head.

"Detective, we have a small group of regular donors, and Sarah did a wonderful job of keeping them happy while cultivating new ones. She was always polite, not too pushy, but followed through, and got us the checks. Our expanded curriculum and scholarship program, case in point."

"Do you know if she was friendlier with some than others?"

Borderline, Dakota observed as the woman's eyes narrowed.

"What are you implying?"

"Nothing," Rachel said. "I imagine people who invest a lot of money might feel...entitled sometimes. They might prefer one program over another. Sarah spent a lot of time engaging with them, so is it possible that someone felt entitled to more of her time than she was willing to give to them?"

She kept the same friendly, conversational tone, almost hypnotic as the dean's anger seemed to dissolve. Dakota was still annoyed at the general situation, though she did like her voice. A lot.

"If that happened, and I can't imagine it did, Sarah never mentioned anything. She was professional through and through, and everyone who worked with her knew it. We miss her terribly."

"I'm sorry for your loss," Rachel said softly. "I'm going to need a list of those donors, and her calendar. I suppose there's a copy among your records. We could come back with a warrant, but you know how it goes. It will be faster if we can check right away, and I promise we'll be as discreet as necessary."

"I don't want to hold you up," the dean said with a sigh. "I'll have my assistant print it out for you."

"Thank you. We appreciate it."

Dakota couldn't believe what she was hearing. And she couldn't believe how she, no stranger to fundraisers and entitled donors, had overlooked this. No, not overlooked. They had interviewed Sarah's co-workers, and nothing suggested that the murder was connected to her job.

When they walked back to the car—with the list and Sarah's work calendar—Dakota asked,

"Why the donors?" Her tone held both admiration and envy, emotions she would have preferred to keep to herself. Rachel didn't seem to notice or care.

"There's lots of money involved. And ego. Most murders come down to that, don't you think?"

Dakota pondered her words. "She might have been sleeping with someone. Wife or girlfriend got jealous?"

"Or Sarah found out something about a donor they wanted to stay hidden, and they wanted to silence her," Rachel countered. "We can't jump to conclusions. I want to see if anyone in that group has access to pharmaceuticals and knowledge in chemistry. Not that it takes a lot of knowledge to know that rat poison can kill a person, but the right dose at the right time?"

"Makes sense," Dakota acknowledged. Grudgingly, but still. "We'll look into that. You wanted to see the crime scene?"

"Yes. It won't take long. I just want to get an impression, then we can head back."

Burton was making her nervous. Dakota didn't like being nervous, especially around an older colleague, she reflected. She had worked hard to prove to everyone that she belonged where she was, to her parents, her boss, co-workers, and even the criminals she had put away.

What was even more disconcerting was the idea that she might have a blind spot. Why hadn't she thought about the university's donors? Because her parents' names were on that list?

Rachel hadn't mentioned it yet, but Dakota had no illusions—she would.

So much for keeping a low profile at work. The drive to Cooper's home was once more made in awkward silence. Dakota was too aware of her new colleague next to her, the scent of her perfume, her hands on the steering wheel. Nothing but distractions, and she had no use for those. She was aware of them, but nonetheless frustrated with herself. She needed to prove herself, be professional, especially around Burton. She took a sharp breath, not surprised to see Rachel stifle a smile. Dakota had to be careful, for many reasons. She forced her thoughts back to the case.

Everything about it felt wrong. Had she started her investigation from the wrong angle?

Much as Mark admired her, Rachel Burton couldn't do magic, could she?

As few minutes later, Dakota watched as Rachel walked around the room where Sarah Cooper had died. Her surroundings suggested that she'd been comfortable financially. Even the basement was nicely furnished, open doors revealing a bathroom to one side, and a laundry room to the other.

Dakota's gaze went back to the small window that was almost on level with the ground upstairs. Sarah's taste for decoration was a bit quirky for a woman her age, but all the quirky items had been dusted for prints and examined thoroughly. No hidden messages anywhere.

"What's with the creepy dolls in the window?" Rachel asked.

Dakota shrugged. "No collectors' items. We checked. No prints on either of them either. There are a few weird items on the shelves, so this fit. A childhood memento maybe, or something she got from her grandmother. There are some old-fashioned porcelain dishes in the cabinets upstairs. With her dad being an abusive ass and the mom pretty much raising her single, she spent a lot of time with the grandmother. Makes sense she kept this."

"In the basement though."

"Fits with the rest, no?"

"Hm."

"What does that mean?" She told herself not to raise her voice, not to get into an argument on day one. That moment might come soon enough. Focus. They were here to solve the case, justice for Sarah Cooper. Her questions could wait.

"I don't know yet. Let's go back and work on that list, shall we? Oh, and Lord. Are you by any means related?"

She knew this was coming.

"Yeah, I think we can scratch them off the list. I'll talk to them, but I can't imagine Mom and Dad came up with a nefarious scheme to kill Sarah Cooper."

"You never met her?"

Rachel held her gaze, dead serious about her question.

"Where are you going with this? No, I never met her. I attended that university, but Sarah wasn't working there at the time. And I'm not involved with my parents' donations. We should go back."

"Sure."

It was only afternoon. This would be a series of long days.

"What are you doing?" Dakota asked when Rachel pulled into the parking lot of a coffee shop.

"I don't know about you, but I had an early breakfast. I need something to eat. You're not hungry?"

Dakota was about to deny, but her rumbling stomach gave her away.

"I guess I could use something," she admitted. She was still nervous. This had to stop. Maybe a coffee and something sweet would calm her nerves.

This time, Rachel didn't hide the smile.

Too many emotions, too many inappropriate thoughts flickering through her brain. None of them mattered, Dakota told herself. They were here for one thing, and one thing only.

Besides, she wasn't willing to forgive her. Resentment would facilitate distance, and that was a good thing.

Chapter 3

S arah's murderer might not be on the list of donors, and Rae had no problem scratching Dakota Lord's parents off it—but she was curious. She still thought that someone among these men and women had some vital information for them. They might not even know it yet. And she still believed that her theory was the better one. She didn't say it out loud, sensing that the younger detective was not entirely happy with the way the day had gone.

It made Rae even more curious about her, her family, and how they were connected to Sarah's workplace.

Tomorrow was another day. She thought they had made good progress, and if she headed home early enough, she might be able to catch Genevieve and Simon—well, Gen, anyway. She might have to wait for the weekend to see Simon, or perhaps she could sneak away during a lunch break.

No regrets, she told herself as she shrugged into her coat. She had chosen this, had known that it might come with a less convenient schedule. The general idea was that she only had to manage her own time from now on—the reality of it might look slightly different, but she would adapt.

If nothing else, Rae was brilliant at adapting.

"Burton, hey. A few of us are going for a drink, would you like to join us?" Baker, one of the other detectives, asked.

That was extremely early, and she still had a chance to make that call...

"Not tonight, I'm sorry. Maybe closer to the weekend."

"Can't party on a school night?" Dakota's amusement was obvious. "I could use a drink," she told Baker. "Have a good night, Rachel."

Rae decided she could be offended or take the advice her therapist and everyone had given her when she complained about being lonely—cry herself to sleep around nine p.m. less often. Socialize. Rachel wasn't crying anymore, but there were still lots of early nights. Well, she had her reasons.

Didn't everyone?

"Wait," she called after her colleagues, both of them turning to her. "I could do one drink. It's my first day, so...I'll pay."

Socialize, not try to buy friends, she heard her therapist. No. She was introducing herself to a new group, and while she wouldn't push to make friends, she knew that this kind of gesture went a long way. Maybe she could figure out why Dakota disliked her this much.

The place was simply called The Tavern, and it was only a few blocks away from the harbor. No water view, but lots of maritime décor. It was cozy enough, Rae decided, and she wouldn't come to regret her decision. The drinks written in chalk on a blackboard reflected a rather medium-priced menu, and everyone went for beers.

Fairly tame.

"You come here often?" she asked. Rae didn't know what to make of the smile curling Dakota's lips, as if she'd said something funny.

Detective Baker was blissfully oblivious to the continued tension in the air.

"Once, twice a week maybe," he said. "It's close, it's convenient. And sometimes we just don't want to go home right away."

"I get that, believe me." Today, it wasn't because of a case, though the atmosphere of Sarah Cooper's basement, death, quirky mementos, creepy dolls, and rat poison, had stayed with her. Rae didn't like ambiguity, in her personal or professional life. If there was something going on between the lines, she wanted to clear the air.

And perhaps, for once, Genevieve could wait, because she certainly hadn't asked Rae's opinion before making more far-reaching decisions than skipping a call.

A couple of other officers she recognized from earlier joined them, and the evening proceeded with familiar shop talk. Most of them didn't seem to mind or question her presence in any way. There was always more work to do, and every addition to the team helped. No need to look any further, was there?

She was aware that Dakota seemed to have a different approach. Rae caught her glances every once in a while, somewhere between curious and frustrated. She probably didn't think it was that obvious, but Rae had perfected the skill of reading people who were judging her—as a cop, as a mother and partner. Dakota had no idea.

They didn't see her coming, Mark had said. Well, Rae came with her own set of skills. She could understand that Dakota wasn't too happy about having been assigned a partner on this case, though she could simply get over her ego and be grateful. Two pairs of eyes seeing more than one and all, and whatever trace might have been there, it was already getting cold. There was no time to be territorial. She had experienced that enough with male cops, even Mark, and found it somewhat disappointing, if that was the problem the younger detective had.

But it was hardly the only problem. Earlier, Rae had stolen away to the breakroom for a few minutes and done some quick research. She didn't know anyone in the Lord family in person, but of course she had heard of them.

This opened a whole new set of theories about her temporary partner. The Lords were, as Dakota had hinted, on the moderate part of the continuum, which these days, Rae assumed could mean a lot of things. They were engaged in many charities, most of them leaning conservative. And they gave a lot of money to the university.

Dakota could have done anything, yet she chose this job. It was interesting. It was none of her business, she reflected.

"So, you got any stories about Castillo he doesn't want us to know about?" Baker asked with a grin.

"Well…that depends on the stories he's told you about me," she countered, making everyone at the table laugh. Everyone except…Dakota barely smiled. Rae was beginning to get equally frustrated with her. "To be honest, there's nothing to tell. He's a good guy. By the book. But you know that already."

"He's a pretty good boss," Dakota said after taking a sip of her beer.

Rae had a brief confusing moment of focusing on her lips.

"I heard that you used to be one."

"I had a different rank, that's true. But just in case that was ever a question, it was my choice. I wanted to go back to working cases. It's what I'm good at, and I knew Mark was looking for someone. So…Here I am."

For better or worse, whether you like it or not.

"I think that's great," Baker said. "We need more hands on deck, less politics. We know how to do the job."

"Yeah. We certainly do." Dakota slipped from her chair and picked up her phone and coat. "I'll see you tomorrow. Thanks for the beer."

"No prob—"

She was already gone. Rae stared after her for a split-second before she decided she wasn't going to let this stand. Ambiguity—she really hated it, and she couldn't let it hinder the work. Both she and Mark needed to convince the Powers That Be that their decisions had been the right ones, not made on a whim. The outcome of these efforts, and the creepy doll case, could determine their careers. Creepy doll case? When had she started to call it that?

Priorities. Dakota might be as good as everyone said, but she still had a lot to learn.

"Wait a second?" she called after her, catching up at the front door.

Dakota turned around, her expression unreadable.

"It's late," she said.

"Yet you were the one joking about partying on a school night. I think you can handle a few more minutes."

"Okay." She leaned back against the wooden beam. "What do you want to talk about?"

She was stubborn, irritating. Beautiful. That was beside the point, and, Rae thought, likely a reflection of her own envy. Why did she have to explain herself at every turn for something that was one hundred percent logical?

"What's your problem with me?"

That might have been a little over the top, but she did get a reaction. Not the answer she had hoped for though.

"Why do you think I have a problem with you? Castillo made his decision. Is it the right one? We'll see, but that's done. I just want to get the job done."

"Same here. You're sure there's nothing else?"

That earned her a sigh. "There's nothing else. I'm sorry, okay? It's been a rough week. Let's leave it at that."

"If I can do anything…"

"Thanks. Good night, Rachel."

"You can call me Rae."

"So, we're friends now? All right then." With a laugh, she walked away, making Rae regret she'd made that offer. She hoped this conversation would be enough. She didn't want to be the newbie who complained about a partner during the first week.

You have to learn to relax, she heard Genevieve's voice in her head. Just great.

She went back to the table to say goodbye as well.

Rae let herself into her apartment to Rex's accusatory meowing.

"Yeah, I know. I am the worst mom," she told him, and he didn't seem to disagree. Figures. She made a quick job of emptying his litter box and providing fresh food and water. "You didn't even finish what I gave you this morning."

He gave her a long stare before turning to walk away, only to be back in a heartbeat when she got out the treats. "Right. You love me after all because I control the treats." She sat on her living room couch, and Rex, having a moment of forgiveness, curled up next to her.

They had become reluctant allies when they had no choice, because all the decisions had been made without them.

When Genvieve decided that Simon was old enough for a pet. When she decided that Simon should see more of the world, and she took that job in Paris. She took their son with her, not the pet though, so Rae who wasn't a cat person, and a proud Abyssinian who had loved Simon more than any human, had to make it work. So far so good. Missing the two people who had brought them together was at least something they shared.

Too wired to sleep and knowing she was going to regret this, Rae opened another beer, because truth be told she was only now starting to wind down.

No matter how assured she'd been in her decision, it hadn't been real until now.

That meant the divorce was real too. She was officially a single woman, no longer a lieutenant, and free to do whatever she wanted, even if that was having a beer at eleven. On a school night, she scoffed.

She couldn't figure her out, and it bothered her. It didn't seem to be ignorance, or ageism specifically. But whatever it was, Rae worried it wasn't solved yet.

Up early after a night with little sleep, she caught Genevieve's call this time. Talk about envy. Her ex was having a late lunch in a Parisian café, complete with sunlight and blue skies. Rae cast a look outside her window streaked by rain.

"Hey! How's it going? How was your first day?"

"Fine. I guess." She wouldn't go into finer details and potential complications, certain that Gen didn't want to hear about them.

"That's...understated."

"No, I'm serious. It's been good. It's what I wanted."

"Well, I'm happy for you then."

"Thanks. What about Simon? Can I talk to him later?"

Genevieve's regretful gaze already told her the answer before she spoke.

"I'm sorry, Rae, he's really busy this week. School, soccer, extracurricular art program and friends...I promise we'll make time on the weekend."

She'd have to leave in ten minutes, not enough time to start an argument, though she wanted to. She knew that Gen wasn't keeping Simon from her on purpose. That had never been the plan because she wasn't that kind of person. But Rae missed him badly, and perhaps there was a part of her that worried he might like all those people better than her, eventually forget about her.

"Send me some pictures then, okay? And let him know he can always call me. I'll make the time."

"I know that." Her tone sounded both apologetic and offended, if that was possible. "He knows that."

They both should, Rae reflected, because for years, her decisions, career and otherwise, had been solely based on making sure that she could spend enough time with them. Go up the ladder as quickly as possible, get the safer, better-paying job.

"I'll wait for pictures, then. I'm jealous of your coffee and pastry."

Genevieve smiled. "Doesn't take a detective to determine that."

Damn, she still missed her too.

"I know you just started your new job, and that you'll be busy, but once you can take a vacation, why don't you come visit us in Paris? I'd love to show you around, and you could spend time with Simon."

Genevieve had grown up in a small town near Paris. Her offer was tempting in many ways, and yet, she had summarized all the reasons, the main reason why Rae couldn't do anything like that right now.

"I'll see what I can do." Of course she wanted to see Simon. Of course, she couldn't take a vacation when she'd just made a huge detour in her career and needed some time to determine how it would pan out. Being in Paris with Gen would be...complicated. Dangerous. "I'll see you on the weekend," she said. "When you find a time that works for you, text me, and I'll make sure I'm free."

"Great. Enjoy your day."

She'd try.

"You too."

Rae finished her toast and coffee while Rex studied her with curiosity, probably waiting for more treats.

Chapter 4

In the past ten days, Dakota Lord had arrived at the station before any of the other colleagues in her unit   sometimes, like today, even before Mark Castillo. She liked this period to prepare and deal with any possible distractions. Like the fact that her parents were on a list of names she hadn't even thought to ask for.

Dakota didn't think that any of the university's direct donors were involved in Sarah Cooper's death. This wasn't their MO. If they wanted someone gone, they'd destroy their reputation and hound them out of town, in a subtle polite way. Not murder.

The dolls. Yes, they were bizarre, but not more bizarre than some of the other knickknacks Sarah had collected, a mix of travel mementos and other items from her past.

Dakota sipped the latte she had brought from her favorite coffee shop on the way, suppressing a sigh as she admitted that the most complicated distraction was, or would be, sitting across from her.

As if she had summoned her, Rae Burton walked through the double doors, her own coffee in hand. There was probably not much they could bond over, except a shared caffeine addiction.

Why would she even need to bond? This was going to be temporary, the partnership at least. Rae's future in this unit was yet to be determined, but Dakota didn't intend to stay here forever.

"Morning," Rae mumbled as she settled behind her desk.

Not a morning person then.

Dakota reflected on last night's interaction. She remembered her own disbelief when Castillo told them about the new addition to the unit. It was no secret to anyone around here that he held Rachel Burton in high regard. Rae this, Rae that.

After observing her for only a day, Dakota could admit that there must be some truth to the stories, regardless, her disappointment hadn't abated.

"Good morning to you," she said, hoping Rae wouldn't prod any more. She had enough on her plate. That was not a conversation she wanted to have.

Rae looked up from the papers of her desk.

"Of the four families Sarah contacted in the week she died, one appointment was canceled a day before. She might have lost the university a big amount of money."

"The dean didn't mention it." Dakota sighed. "To save Sarah's reputation? Or to save face?"

"We don't know yet, but I'd like to talk to them."

"You still want to go down that avenue?"

There was a hint of surprise in Rae's expression. "Unless you have a better idea."

It was somewhat implied that Dakota didn't, the accusation tickling her temper.

"Look, I know that Mark sees you as some sort of miracle worker, good for you, but you've been on this case for one day. Let me breathe a little, will you?"

She regretted her words instantly. She never wanted to be the woman who had a problem working with another woman, especially when she was more experienced. Dakota didn't have any problem with more experienced women whatsoever. Usually.

Rae Burton was special in so many ways.

"Sure. Whatever you like. Are you going to come with me? I can do this alone if you prefer."

"No. Forget about it. I'm coming."

"Good."

"You want to announce the visit?"

With a smile, Rae shook her head. "No. I don't want to give them time to prepare a story. This," she lifted her badge, "will be enough to let us in. People like that think they're doing us a favor talking to us."

"People like that?" She wasn't wrong, and still her choice of words didn't sit right with Dakota. Anyone who willingly took a cut in their paycheck like Rae had, certainly wasn't poor. She didn't have any talking room.

"I didn't mean anything by it. Let's go."

"Wherever you were planning to go, that will have to wait."

Castillo's serious tone sent a shiver down Dakota's spine. This wasn't good. She knew before he spoke.

"There's been another one. We call it a suspicious death for now, but I hate to say most of it looks like a carbon copy of Cooper."

Rae swore quietly.

"I still want to circle back to the Bedfords later," she said. "Depending on how long this takes, we'll push it to tomorrow."

She had an easy way of taking charge, Dakota noticed, something she found both irritating and, God help her, attractive. None of it mattered though because they had another suspicious death, likely murder, to solve.

Carbon copy might have been a bit exaggerated, but the similarities were uncanny, to put it mildly.

For the second time in less than two weeks, Dakota was crouching next to the body of a woman in her thirties, cause of death...She had her suspicions. Marla Peters had been found by her sister in what was another finished basement, though the house was much smaller than the first victim's. In the latter's case, the woman who came twice a week to clean had found the body.

Like Sarah, Marla Peters wore PJs. Dakota noted that her hair was in two braids. Like Sarah's had been.

Her gaze fell on the single window letting in some of the morning sun. A window going out to the street, on the sill...The sight turned her stomach.

There could be no doubt now.

"Yeah. This is fucked up," Rae said next to her. "That means Sarah might not have been the first, and if we're not fast enough, there could be others. And, whoever did this now wants us to know that he killed them both."

"Sleeping pills and rat poison."

"I'd prefer if you waited until after the autopsy to draw those conclusions," a friendly voice reminded her. Tanner, the new medical examiner, was about her age, looking more like he'd stepped out of GQ than like someone who was around dead bodies all day. He had hit on her once but quickly realized she wasn't interested and backed off.

"Well, I think she's right," Rae said. "And I'm pretty sure neither Sarah nor Marla bought any of those dolls. Look. He sat them in a way that they look outside the window."

Abruptly, she left the room, and Dakota had no choice but to hurry after her. Rae left the house and went to the street where they could see the basement window.

The dolls, four this time, were staring back at them.

Dakota thought back to coming to the scene of the first murder that they knew of. Tanner's caution aside, she was quite sure that they were dealing with another one. She had seen the dolls, though the way they sat in the window didn't seem all that important when they still assumed they had belonged to Sarah. Someone might have moved them slightly while brushing for prints.

Another guess: They wouldn't find any fingerprints on these either.

"You knew they were important right away." She wished that her mixed emotions, envy and admiration, didn't come across so clearly in her tone. Apparently, she had a hard time keeping her words and feelings to herself around her new partner.

"Don't worry about it," Rae told her. "You documented everything in painstaking detail. That made it easy to find something that stood out."

Was that a compliment? Somewhat backhanded?

"What is the connection?" she asked out loud. "We have to check if there's any relation to the university."

"Sister says she worked at the mall but took evening classes. That's a yes."

"Okay. But that doesn't have anything to do with the donors."

"We'll see. I really want to know where those dolls came from."

"They're not anything special," Dakota reminded her. "They're the kind you can find in any toy store, and online of course. If our perp wants to keep killing, I don't think he would get them at a local store."

"If the perp is a he, but I agree that it's more likely. It would make sense that he would buy the dolls online." Rae paused for a moment. However, I think there are things he does want us to know. We'll start with that."

Dakota mulled over her words. Sarah Cooper's autopsy had shown no signs of sexual assault. Poison as the weapon of choice. Those could still point to a woman—or someone who wanted them to believe that. And the dolls, what did they represent? The M.O. of a ritualistic killer, something tied to his childhood, his victims', or both? Or was he simply giving them the finger?

"When we're done here, let's go get a coffee," she said. "I have some ideas."

Chapter 5

"She would never buy those! They're hideous!" was the reaction of Marla's sister when they showed her the pictures of the dolls. Rae and Dakota had made a stop at her work, a clothes retailer.

That might be a strong word to describe them. Nevertheless, the distraught woman was unwittingly confirming the pattern.

"Just to make sure, you've never seen them before," Dakota said. She now spoke softly, her tone having an impact. On Rae too, but she forced herself to focus.

"No, never. She had better taste than that, and it's definitely nothing we played with as children."

No matter the angle, the implications of this case were all dire, Rae thought after they finished the conversation. The only neighbor they had managed to talk to so far couldn't contribute anything. He claimed to have hardly seen her at all. They would have to come back to speak to others.

On their way back, they stopped at a coffee shop. Rae kept her thoughts to herself while they were standing in line, and not just because she was distracted by the scent of Dakota's perfume. Nothing on her mind was suitable for public consumption at this moment. Once they sat in a booth, she opted to share her thoughts on their progress.

"He's careful. I don't think there'll be any prints on those dolls either."

"I agree," Dakota said.

That, together with the coffee and double chocolate donut in front of her—some clichés had truth to them—was a small silver lining, and Rae would take any she could get. She had taken to a healthier lifestyle when Gen and Simon had been with her every day, and she didn't intend on letting it all lapse, but given how her week was going, she felt entitled. At least Dakota hadn't commented on that though she had gone with a turkey sandwich. After putting whatever pieces they had so far, together, they would go see Mr. and Mrs. Bedford, the donors that had canceled their appointment with Sarah Cooper.

They drank their coffee in silence for a minute or so before Dakota asked, "Have you ever seen anything like this before?"

It made Rae wonder how much of a guess this really was—or how many stories Mark had shared with his unit.

"Once," she said. "It wasn't about dolls or anything, and they weren't all women."

"Was there a connection to the perp's childhood?"

"No. He was just an asshole trying to play us...not that it would have been an excuse. Sometimes there is no other explanation."

"But it would help us to find the pattern."

"Certainly. So far, we have the dolls. The university, the basement—a bit more luxurious in Sarah's case, but the principle is the same. Both found by people who were in their lives regularly, so he didn't want to hide the bodies from us for long."

"Comfy PJs," Dakota added. "I don't know about you, but I dress like that when I don't expect anyone. He must have known how to get into the house unseen."

"Yeah."

"The braids, however. I had hair like that last in fourth grade or so."

"He kills them, braids their hair and puts the dolls on the windowsill?" Rae shuddered, and not just because Dakota had brought up that old story. The idea that she might own one of those PJs with cats on them was definitely more pleasant, but probably even more inappropriate.

Probably?

She could feel the heat rise up her body, all the way to her face. Damn perimenopause.

"The poison takes a little time to take effect," Dakota reminded her. "So how does he pull that off?"

"Beats me. Shall we head to the Bedfords now?"

"Sure."

Rae walked after her, a bit envious and resentful of her colleague for whom hot flashes were a thing of a distant future. She took a deep breath. She needed to think less about her colleague and more about the right questions to ask the Bedfords.

She hadn't expected Mr. and Mrs. Bedford to be quite so accommodating. They had both of them sit in the den, and Mrs. Bedford offered coffee which they politely declined.

Rae didn't have any illusions. Every item, every piece of furniture and square inch of this place screamed luxury, something that made Sarah's home seem modest. If they gave millions to the university, it was more than a statement. They also gave to conservative causes.

She was intrigued, however, by the way they greeted Dakota.

"Ms. Lord, it's a pleasure. We haven't seen you in such a long time."

Dakota, on the edge of her seat, gave a terse smile.

"It's good to see you too, Mrs. Bedford. Unfortunately, we still have to ask a few questions...about Sarah."

"Yes, poor Sarah, such a tragedy," Mr. Bedford said. "How can we help?"

"Sarah had an appointment with you to discuss the funding of a new program at the university," Rae said. "We learned that it was canceled. Can you tell us why?"

She wasn't sure what to make of his puzzled expression.

"I don't see how that could be important, but I think...Sarah retracted her invitation. I'm not sure what the reason was, but you'd have to ask my children. They are more involved in the donations. Sometimes it's good not to know what they spend my money on."

Rae didn't find the joke particularly well-timed, given that they were talking about a young woman's death, but she gave him a smile anyway, wanting him to be comfortable.

Beside her Dakota seemed to have trouble sitting still, brimming with nervous energy.

"Well, it would be helpful if we could gain some insight into it. You have a son and a daughter, isn't that right? Who should we talk to in this matter?"

"They are on a business trip at the moment and will be back next week."

Nice try.

"Could you give us a cell phone number so we could join them?"

He frowned. "I'm not sure I'm comfortable with where this is going. Shouldn't we wait until they are back, and we can invite our lawyers to the conversation?"

That was more like it, true colors and all.

Rae shook her head, keeping the polite smile frozen on her face.

"We just need to ask some questions," Dakota said, sounding impatient.

"My colleague is right. They might be able to help us with some information. That's all." Rae hoped that they would believe her. She knew from experience how some of those important conversations were stymied at an early stage by lawyers and paranoia.

"I guess we can do that..." Mrs. Bedford sounded unsure.

"You don't have to worry about anything. I'll talk to Mona."

"I'm surprised you don't have her number already." Gone was the polite tone from Mr. Bedford's voice, replaced by an almost sneer.

Rae sat up straighter, startled.

"But I guess you burned a lot of bridges, Dakota. It's no secret that your parents are worried."

"My parents have nothing to worry about. Could you give us that number now? Otherwise, we'll be back on Monday. We could always go directly to the cell phone companies..."

Rae held back, knowing that this would be at best a doomed fishing expedition, but it seemed to do the trick.

Dakota held out her phone, and Mrs. Bedford typed in the numbers.

"Thank you so much for your time," Rae told them. "Just one more thing. Do you know this woman?"

"No, I've never seen her," Mrs. Bedford said after studying Marla Peters' picture.

"No, never. Who is she?" Mr. Bedford asked.

"Are you sure?" Dakota asked.

"Yes, absolutely."

"Thanks," Rae said again.

She wondered what it was about this environment that made Dakota cranky and defensive. After two days, it was hard to determine, but maybe that was her default personality.

No. She'd seen her act differently too, thoughtful and compassionate with the victim's sister, another time, joking with a colleague.

So, she was only this reserved with Rae, and friends of her parents from whom she seemed somewhat estranged. Interesting.

Back in the car, they drove to the station in the hope of more pieces of the puzzle awaiting them.

"Well, we got the numbers. They're only an hour ahead of us, so we could make these calls right away."

"I'll take care of it."

"I don't mind calling—"

"I said I'll take care of it."

"Right. Okay."

The rest of the drive was made in silence. Once they arrived, Dakota picked up her phone while Rae went to see the medical examiner.

She was none the wiser...about many things, but she knew for certain that since this morning they had a much bigger problem. She still wished she could figure out what Dakota Lord's was.

Dakota had left for home when Rae turned off her computer and put on her coat, her mind still occupied with the day's events. No prints on the dolls. Two women poisoned in their home.

What was the message behind all this?

"Rae. I was just about to head for dinner. Would you like to join me?"

She gave Castillo a quizzical look. "Are you asking as my boss?"

"As your friend. Maybe as your boss too, but don't worry. I have to admit I wasn't sure about this, but you seem to be adjusting fine."

"Seem to be? Come on, Mark, you don't have to buy me dinner to break the news. What's the matter?"

He burst into laughter. "Who said I was buying? I'll meet you at Victor's in twenty minutes. They still have the best burgers in town."

Rae shook her head but didn't comment. He at least was a reliable ally. Everyone else was polite, except...but that was a subject for another day.

"I can't miss out on that. All right."

They parted ways in the parking lot, and a short drive later, she was sitting across from her former partner, enjoying a meal every bit as fabulous as she remembered. It was making her a bit nostalgic. They had talked a lot about their hopes and aspirations—and they'd both made it, except Rae had made decisions that seemed to be hard to understand for everyone around her.

"It's been quite the start," she admitted, "but like you said, I'm adjusting. You know I'm not a newbie in all this. You can trust me."

"Oh, of course, I know. You'll be fine." He took a sip of his beer. "I wanted to talk to you about Dakota."

Part of her might have anticipated the subject, but he still caught her off guard by going there straight away.

"I'm not sure I'm comfortable with this. I'm doing my job, she's doing hers. That's all."

"Sure. I just wanted you to know where she's coming from. If her first instinct is to do things alone it's because she had to for most of her life. Don't worry, this is as far as I'll go, but it's no secret that her parents didn't approve of her choices."

"She has a lot to prove," Rae concluded. "I get it. I've been there."

"I knew you'd understand," he said, sounding relieved. "The Lords cast quite the shadow in this town. It's hard to get out from under that."

"Trust fund and all."

"Rae."

"I know. I'm sorry. I'll keep in mind what you said. Now, do they still have that lemon meringue pie here?"

"You bet," he said. "But first tell me what your impression is. Are we looking at more murders?"

"I'll do everything I can to prevent that."

They both knew what that meant.

"Whatever resources you need, you name it. We need to put a stop to this."

Rae couldn't agree more. Her mind was clear where the case was concerned, and even more confused when it came to Dakota. Maybe that, too, meant something. Or perhaps, once this case was over, she had to create an online dating profile like Gen had hinted at.

Chapter 6

The younger Bedfords confirmed that Sarah had canceled the appointment but insisted that it had in no way impacted their professional relationship. They had meant to reschedule, then the business trip came up and Sarah never got back to them.

Dakota sighed when she saw the incoming text from her mother, no doubt chiding her for questioning the Bedford family. There was a reason why she and parents didn't talk often—polite agree-to-disagree could only go so far.

She parked her car in the parking garage and sat for a few minutes.

If Rae wasn't already here, she certainly would be within a short time. Some details Mark hadn't talked about, but Dakota had found out about her anyway: She was divorced. Her son and ex-wife lived in Paris.

Dakota would have loved to go, just drop everything, and hop on a plane. Technically, she could, but it was exactly that fact that stopped her from doing it. It wouldn't feel like she earned it.

Of course, her parents would have never wanted her to just live the luxury life while squandering her trust fund, but they would have liked her to have a career in a more prestigious profession. Like one of those lawyers Bedford had talked about.

Dakota believed in the law, but she had always wanted something that mattered more than making rich people richer and shielding them from accountability. She wanted to prove that she could make it on her own, just like Rae Burton had before...Well, life had given both of them detours.

Dakota couldn't seem to escape her parents' influence no matter where she turned. Rae...That was a different story. She had made choices. None of Dakota's business, for sure, but still frustrating.

One day, maybe, she would tell Rae.

Before heading for her desk, she went to the morgue where she knew ME Graham to be at work already. She found him in his office, enjoying a cup of coffee as he was typing at his computer.

Dakota wasn't particularly queasy, but once she walked past these doors, even in the office she couldn't imagine tolerating any sort of food or drink, not even a black coffee.

"Detective Lord, good morning. You're here to ask about Marla Peters, I assume."

"You assume correctly."

She found herself smiling despite the dire circumstances. Well, they were always dire down here, but Graham never seemed to lose his optimistic disposition. Perhaps you had to have one doing the job he did. Dakota preferred to be cautious to the point of jaded as it was the stereotype for *her* profession. It had served her well so far.

"I guess you won't be surprised when I tell you that most of everything looks exactly the same it did in the Sarah Cooper case. Last meal was dinner with a glass of wine, and somewhere around that time she ingested a cocktail of sleeping pills and rat poison."

"What a crappy way to go," Dakota commented.

"Can't argue with you on that."

The perp had taken Sarah's phone, or so they assumed. From her bills they knew that she had one, but it had been turned off the day of her death. Like Marla, she had no landline.

She listened to his preliminary findings, struggling not to get distracted by her own thoughts as she imagined the women's last moments—hours.

The poison took some time to take effect, but by the time they realized something was wrong, it was too late? Could they have called 911?

Not if he took their phones first.

She had concluded that the murderer had to have cleaned up the room some, because they didn't find any used dishes or take-out containers, no open bottle of wine.

Okay, so she hadn't caught the dolls, but she had made a note about the basement. Yes, it was a finished space, but why would they be there on an ordinary evening—having dinner in their PJs?

"And here's the good news," Graham said, sounding pleased. "We didn't find any prints on the dolls, and whoever did this, was extremely careful...but this time, we have a hair. Still have to run some analysis, but—"

"DNA? I could kiss you."

"Come on, Lord, we both know you won't. You might want to kiss the sexy new tech who found it, but that's beside the point."

"Yeah. It sure is. Thank you."

"You're very welcome. Would you like a coffee?"

Yes, but not here.

"No thanks. I'll talk to you later. Let me know as soon as you have anything else."

"Of course."

She headed upstairs, feeling some of the pressure lift for the first time since she'd started working on this case. Despite what Rae might think, she didn't have a problem sharing the credit. The faster they solved this the better.

This time, she didn't even mind seeing her at her desk, papers spread out in front of her.

"Come with me," she said. "We have to talk to the lieutenant."

"We have a hair which means a much better chance at identifying the perp. Graham will get back to me on that. Meanwhile, I've been thinking…The ritual might be even more extensive than we thought. Why didn't they have time to call 911? He's not just in it for the killing. He makes sure they are in a certain room, no access to a phone, no way to get help. I think it's not too far off to imagine he might have dinner with them. He might even bring them down to the basement later. He cleans up afterwards and leaves."

Rae didn't say anything.

Lieutenant Castillo had a few points to offer.

"Let's hope the DNA results will yield something useful. As for your theory…Are you saying that we'll have to bring in some outside help?"

That was not at all what she'd meant.

"I think we can crack this case. We can find him before he kills again."

"I, and the rest of the city would sure like you to do so. I strongly agree that this perp will kill again if we don't stop him soon. I'll have Baker give you a hand if needed."

"I'm not sure that will be enough," Rae finally spoke. "The dolls, the extended ritual, more and more points to someone organized. We don't have any prints. DNA will certainly help, but it's circumstantial. We might need the assistance at some point. A real profile."

"I think at this point we can handle..." Dakota stopped when she saw the look passing between Rae and Castillo. So much for not asking any favors.

To her surprise, Rae continued, "For the moment, yes. We will let you know, of course. Good catch," she said to Dakota.

That woman was giving her whiplash. The strangest thing was, even if her job made it impossible to stay away, Dakota wasn't sure she wanted to. It was even stranger that she enjoyed the praise, especially since Rae had chosen to give it in front of their boss.

"All right, thanks," he said. "Now get back to work."

They went back to a quiet bullpen, where a pensive looking Baker sat behind his computer. Dakota saw that Rae had been poring over crime scene photos before. PJs with cats. Braids. But a grown-up dinner with wine.

She had to admit that Rae had a point. Everything was still theory, and some of the pieces still didn't fit together.

The murderer might see women as infantile, but that wasn't anything new or original, sadly for a lot of people who weren't criminals.

Her phone rang, and she picked it up.

"Detective Lord."

"You are working on that case, the woman who was found dead in her basement?" a timid voice asked.

"Yes. Do you have any information on this case?" She was aware that both Rae and Baker had stopped what they were doing to listen.

"I think it must have been her. She came in, someone came after her and yelled at her. She was really shaken. I offered to call the police, but she didn't want me to. I'm Cindy Loman. I work at a coffeeshop here in the mall."

"Thank you so much for calling. Are you at work now?"

"Yes. I'm sorry, I would have come...I wanted to call right away."

"That's good. Can you give me the address? I'll be right there."

Dakota noted that the mall wasn't the same Marla Peters had worked in, but a smaller one further out of town. The pieces were coming together. With a little luck, they'd have a suspect to compare the DNA findings to by the end of the day.

"Let's take a little road trip," she announced.

"You're in a good mood, Lord," Baker commented.

"I am. We're going to catch ourselves a killer."

Rae looked like Dakota's words made her cringe a little. Dakota didn't care. It would be a good day. Perhaps they could sneak in a coffee break once at the shop.

Cindy, the twenty-something barista, spoke to them while she swiftly prepared beverages. Rae and Dakota had used the occasion to order something for themselves. A celebratory mocha didn't seem such an exaggeration because what Cindy told them might advance their case quickly.

"I'm sorry, I don't watch the news much," she said, "but I saw her picture online, and I realized it was her. A man came in after her, and he was bothering her, yelling about how she owed him. I don't know if it was about money. Everyone was watching, and I knew I had to get him out somehow. When I threatened to call the police, he left."

"Do you have cameras in the shop?" Rae asked.

"Yes, of course. I cleared it with my boss already. He said that if that's the guy who killed her, it's important you get it as soon as possible."

"We don't know yet, but he's right. Thank you, Cindy. Is there anything else you remember about him?"

Given the young woman's distraught expression, she suppressed the smile. Video. Best case scenario, facial recognition software would catch him. Sadly, a volatile individual like that might already be on their radar.

For the moment, she drowned out the nagging voice that wondered if someone who chose rat poison to kill someone would be that obvious. But they couldn't ignore this. What did the man think Marla owed him? Sex? A dinner? Her life? Okay. Nothing to smile about, but they were going to get some answers regarding the incident.

"I don't know...I don't think so. Wait! He had a logo on this shirt, something...a kind of car repair shop."

Rae spun around to Dakota who nodded. On top of a folder containing bills, they had found that Marla had recently paid for a repair. That, together with the video and the DNA sample, would be extremely helpful finding the man who had harassed her.

"Do you think he's going to come back?" Cindy asked anxiously.

Rae didn't want to make false promises though her impression was that he'd want to lay low, either because he had caused a scene in a coffee shop, or because he had just murdered someone.

"If he does, call 911 right away," she said. "And if you remember anything else, you can reach me here. Thank you so much, Cindy. This helps a lot."

"Yes, thank you."

They got their coffees to go, heading back with the camera footage on a USB drive in their possession. Dakota Lord was in the best mood Rae had ever seen her, and it made her let down her guard.

"We make a good team after all," she declared.

Dakota's smile didn't quite tell her if she agreed. "That's maybe a bit early. I mean, she called me. We got lucky."

Because we followed the right steps. Rae didn't say it out loud, because she didn't think there was a point. Maybe after this case she could talk to Mark—if Dakota wanted to work alone so badly, perhaps he should let her. Rae had enough experience of her own to work cases, and if Dakota wanted her help, she could ask for it...She still had a lot of jumbled emotions regarding her younger colleague, and Rae was inclined to blame it all on the confusing past months. Or perimenopause—but she would take today's win.

Before the end of their shift, they could put a name to the face of the man berating what looked like a frightened Marla Peters in the coffee shop. Cindy was in the frame too, trying to deescalate the situation. The camera quality wasn't splendid, but good enough to identify one Damian Hodge, an employee of Complete Car Service.

They caught him at the end of his shift as he was about to leave the building.

"Mr. Hodge," Dakota showed him her badge. "I'm Detective Lord, this is Detective Burton. It's important that we speak to you."

Rae noticed him looking Dakota up and down before he answered.

"What did I do?"

"You're not accused of anything, but you might be able to help us. Let's take this to the station?"

"Should I get a lawyer?"

"You're not under arrest either. We'd just like to ask you a few questions."

Again, he gave Dakota a leering glance. She held his gaze unflinchingly.

"Sure, ladies. Since you ask so nicely."

That was the easy part.

Asked about Marla Peters in the interrogation room later, he denied knowing her.

"That's interesting, because we know you fixed her windshield last week."

"I did?" He looked much too comfortable, leaning back in his seat. "Sorry. I don't remember all the names."

"You remembered her though," Dakota returned. She showed him a short portion of the video on her phone. "That's you, isn't it?"

"Hm...Looks like me. But the quality isn't great, so it's hard to tell."

"It's not that bad," Rae snapped, fed up with his attitude. "You've been in here five minutes, Mr. Hodge, and you're already lying to us. That makes me think you have other things to hide."

He studied her, though didn't quite ogle her the same way.

"Doesn't everyone? But I assume you wanted me to come here for something big."

"What did you mean when you said she owed you?"

He shrugged. "I remember her now. Very flirtatious, that one. I saw her again in the mall and tried to talk to her. She freaked out."

"Strange," Dakota commented. She exchanged a look with Rae before she sat across from Hodge. "I'm afraid that right now, this doesn't look too good for you. In fact, it looks like you're the one who was losing his cool. The barista nearly called the cops on you. You see, our problem with all of this is, a few days after this happened, Marla was murdered."

"What?" He jumped to his feet. "The fuck! I didn't kill any-one!"

"Please, sit down, Mr. Hodge."

Dakota's tone was soft and polite now, and he reacted to it. Hell, Rae reacted to it. She remembered what Mark had told her: *They don't see her coming.*

"I swear this is all some big misunderstanding." He raked a hand through his hair.

Rae could see a bead of sweat forming on his temple.

"She was all nice one moment and then blew me off, okay? No one likes that. I wanted to talk to her, but that woman..." He pointed to Cindy on the screen. "She got all hysterical, so I left. That was the last time I saw Marla. I swear!"

"Then you won't mind submitting to a DNA test, so we can rule you out?"

"I guess not." He sounded unsure now. "Look, I saw her a few times at the shop and then bumped into her at the mall. That's it."

He didn't know that they had found DNA at the scene. If he really was the person who had meticulously cleaned up two basements after committing these murders, he wouldn't assume the police had anything on him, would he? Whoever had left that hair behind wasn't in the system. Damian Hodge wasn't either. Would they match?

"Great. Let's do it then. Give us a few minutes, please?"

When they were on the other side of the two-way mirror, Rae didn't mind sharing her impression.

"You're really good," she said. "I wasn't sure he'd do this so easily."

Dakota shrugged. "He isn't the first. The faster this goes, the better."

"Sure."

What she didn't share was that Dakota's near-seductive tone, directed at Hodge, had almost made her uncomfortable. She knew it was just an act. She also needed to get out more often, and not just with colleagues after work.

"You got any comments, objections?"

When Rae shook her head, Dakota said, "All right. Let's get going. I also want to make sure we can keep an eye on him, because right now there's no way we can hold him."

Rae cast a look at the man behind the window who was nervously wringing his hands in his lap. She wanted to believe that they were close.

"Let me make a few calls," she said.

Chapter 7

Progress. It was a good thing, Dakota reminded herself as they sat in the car in front of Hodge's apartment. So far, nothing was out of the ordinary. He had gone home and stayed in. His car was parked out front, and the light was on in his apartment.

"How did you get this approved so fast?" she asked. If it was a good thing that she was stuck here with Rae for the next few hours, she wasn't sure. At this point, Dakota wasn't sure of much.

Holding on to her grudge had been easy in the beginning, but she had to admit there were things she did appreciate about Rae. She made no secret of the fact that she was comfortable in every possible setting of the job.

But this wasn't just about her, and her own comfort, was it? She studied her profile, suppressing a sigh. There was something about Rae Burton that made it hard to hold on to her righteous disappointment. Part of her resented her for that.

Another part...

"You build a lot of connections over the years," Rae said vaguely.

Maybe she did because she had fit herself into the unit easily. Dakota on the other hand had butted heads and drawn scrutiny on her way up, a lot of which had to do with proving that she was more than her parents' daughter.

She got along well with the guys at work, but she doubted that any of them truly appreciated what was at stake for her beyond the challenges of the day-to-day job.

"If you're lucky."

Rae gave her a quick smile. Dakota felt like she got busted. Someone as meticulous as Rae, and a friend of Mark's, of course she had done her homework on her colleagues too. Dakota wished she could consider her just that, another connection, but Rae was on her mind far too much for that.

She wanted to ask nosy questions. She wanted to...

She hid a yawn behind her hand before she said, "I wonder if he's on to us. It doesn't look like he's leaving home tonight."

"Our guy is careful. Either way he would lay low on the day the cops brought him in."

They went back to silence.

Dakota Lord wasn't a patient person. It didn't sit well with her that she had to wait on multiple things now. Would Damian Hodge reveal himself? By the time another pair of detectives replaced them, and they could leave for their respective homes, he hadn't left.

Dakota assumed that Castillo wouldn't want this to go on for much longer. She hoped that they could get the DNA results back within a reasonable time frame before he decided to skip town, and they wouldn't legally be able to stop him.

As if she wasn't already obsessing enough about Rae Burton, the woman had to be all calm and relaxed about the inevitable delays.

"Experience," Dakota mumbled as she drove to the station the next morning, only a few short hours after they'd parted. She couldn't sleep, or concentrate on much else other than the case, and the breakthrough that might come today. Or not.

She had to admit she was tired, and not just from one long night. Up to this point, her career had been pretty linear. She brought the necessary skills and empathy to succeed, but she was also good at building the kind of rapport with a suspect to make them talk. She had been mocked and yelled at before, but she had never experienced the kind of cat-and-mouse game that this particular perp seemed to enjoy playing.

It shouldn't, but it was getting to her. Rae Burton was getting to her, even though Dakota assumed that she wasn't trying. It was all her, how she somehow got under her skin. At a red light, she leaned back into her seat and sighed.

The timing was all off. There had been a time when she had admired her almost to the point of...what? A crush? They hadn't met before Mark decided to hire her, but Dakota had heard the stories and read about her successes. They had been to some of the same functions but never introduced...until now. Dakota had assumed Rae would have stepped up another rung of the ladder. Instead, they were supposed to be partners. There was so much wrong with that.

When she arrived at the station, Rae wasn't there yet. Castillo was in his office, Baker was frowning at something on his computer screen.

Dakota said hi to him and settled behind her desk, hoping for any important messages from the lab, or Graham, but no such luck.

She picked up the case file and leafed through it again, willing herself to find something they'd missed, something that might help them nail Hodge. Instead, she found her thoughts wandering back to Rae. She was laidback, open-minded, fairly easy to work with. In it for the results, not the glory.

Not to mention...Dakota sighed as she recalled studying her profile while they sat together in the car, just a few hours ago. She was supposed to study the front door instead. Rae hadn't called her out on it, a small smile curving her lips.

Only goes to show, be careful what you wish for. As a uniformed officer, and then as a detective, Dakota had worked alongside men for the biggest part of her career. Partnered with an attractive older woman who knew her way around...many things, who had earned her dues and acted like it? That woman being Rae Burton? It would be a dream if she wasn't so mad at her still. She'd have to get over it too. Even if this was the last case they'd be working on, Rae would be around, making things complicated without even trying.

Things got more complicated soon. Rae came in later in the morning, but since they still didn't have any results, and Hodge had simply gone to work, they still had to wait.

Dakota had used the time to catch up on paperwork, and Rae went to help out Baker with an interrogation. The tension never abated, until that call finally came:

The DNA samples didn't match.

"Thanks anyway," Dakota said, putting down the phone. She knew this might happen, but she hadn't expected feeling this dejected. She hadn't meant to let her emotions show this much, startled when Rae laid a hand on her shoulder.

"It happens," she said softly. "That's not the end of it."

"You think I don't know that? It just makes it so much harder to prove it was him."

"Sure."

Rae withdrew her hand, but the feel of the gentle touch lingered, both comforting and irritating.

"We have to think of something else. It might still be him. Maybe he was that careful. So, the DNA belonged to someone else. Even though everyone swears these women weren't dating, maybe they just did it in secret. The hair could have been planted to stall us."

"Well, that worked. Either way we wasted time."

"We followed a promising lead," Rae corrected her. "That's it. We have to reconsider our options."

Dakota shook her head. "I know what you're trying to do, and I appreciate it, but I'm not a rookie you can comfort with a motivational speech. This is a serious setback!"

"I'm aware of that, Detective Lord. And maybe someone, somewhere, overlooked a detail. Since I've been on this case for less than a week, I assume it wasn't me."

Dakota sat for a few seconds, stunned at the not-so-subtle reproach. She knew she deserved it, pushing and prodding until unshakeable Rae Burton lost her cool. That didn't mean it didn't sting.

As she jumped to her feet to leave the room, she heard Rae direct at Baker, "What are you looking at?" assuming he was about to make a silly cat fight joke.

Nothing funny about this. Once they'd closed this case, she'd take a long vacation, maybe hook up with some random gorgeous, blonde, older woman to fucking get her out of her system.

Chapter 8

Rae regretted the words the moment they came out of her mouth. One of the things she liked most about Dakota Lord was that she was all about the details. Yes, she'd been a bit prickly about the donor list, and she had missed the significance of the dolls, but that could have happened to anyone. Sarah Cooper had eclectic knickknacks all over her place. They couldn't be sure until they had found the other set of dolls at Marla Peters' house.

She'd had her share of getting yelled at by older colleagues, usually men, and she had never wanted to be someone who did it out of spite, especially in front of the team.

She was falling short on a few of her goals, but there was something about Dakota that just set her off. She'd have to find her and apologize. Or set her straight, whichever came first. That night at the bar, she'd let her off the hook too easily.

She left her desk, ignoring Baker's snicker, and went to the breakroom first. A couple of officers were having a snack and a coffee. Next, she went to the bathroom. Sure enough, Dakota stood in front of a mirror, her expression stormy.

"I can't get away from you, can I?"

This time, she didn't take the bait.

"I'm sorry. And I know you're disappointed. I am too. We need to take a good hard look at what we have, move on, but I think there's something we have to do first."

A hint of amusement had replaced suspicion. Jaded didn't quite work on her, Rae reflected. Looking younger than her years, it seemed more like a pout.

"There's nothing that we can do here today. Come with me?"

"Where to, Lieutenant Burton? Excuse me. I mean, Detective."

Rae took a deep breath. She hadn't been wrong to assume that Dakota had a problem. She'd clear it up once and for all, for her peace of mind, and the better of their work.

"You'll just have to trust me."

To her surprise, Dakota followed her silently, though that might be the calm before the storm. They had yet to see, but she was tired and hungry, and at least they'd both get a good meal and reasonably prized booze out of this.

Grace Lydon, the owner, greeted them after they stepped through the door that had a small rainbow flag in one corner.

"Rae, I haven't seen you in a while. How are Gen and Simon?"

Okay, it had been a long while, but she remembered the atmosphere, food, and drinks as extremely comforting. They might even calm Dakota. Speaking of which...She now had an air of curiosity about her.

"Doing well, both of them," Rae hurried to say, while Grace had already turned her attention to her company.

"Hi, I'm Grace. Welcome."

"Thanks. Dakota Lord. Rae and I work together."

"Nice. Come, let me show you your table. Would you like to start with the cocktail of the week?"

"If it has a good amount of booze in it, then yes."

"A snack plate to share?"

"Grace," Rae felt the need to intervene. "Let her see a menu, maybe?"

"That's fine."

Of course, Dakota was being contrary. At this point, Rae had no doubt she was doing it on purpose.

"I was asked to trust, so, yes, the snack plate it is. The place looks great."

It did. Grace had bought an old diner a decade ago and turned it into a cozy bistro-bar where everyone was welcome. On second thought, Rae wasn't sure if it was a good idea to have that necessary conversation in a place that meant a lot to her, but she couldn't back out now.

A few minutes later, they had cocktail glasses with a red and orange drink, and an enormous plate of bar food in front of them. She wished Grace wouldn't wear this knowing smile whenever she came near their table.

She and Dakota had more important things to deal with.

"You got me," the latter said as she picked up a fry. "I feel terrible now."

"That wasn't my intention. You told me everything was all right, but it's clearly not. If we can't work together, we'll have to talk to Mark."

"No. We have to see this through."

"And after that?"

She saw that Dakota had emptied almost half of her glass. If that was what it took to make her talk, Rae wasn't above using questionable methods.

"It's none of my business," Dakota mumbled.

"You seem to be making it your business, and if it affects the work, it's mine too. Let's put it all on the table."

"Fine." Dakota held her gaze, surprising fire in her tone. "You asked for an explanation, I'm going to give you one. What the hell were you thinking? Have you given any thought to how you set women back years?"

"Wait, what?" She couldn't help the laugh, not hiding her disbelief. "I did that single-handedly? How?"

"You're one of the smartest people I know. You figure it out."

"Dakota! What are you talking about?" The trouble was, Rae knew exactly what she was talking about. She had been coping with her own doubts through conversations with Gen, and to a lesser extent, with Mark. She knew that not everyone would understand her decision, and that there might be some ripple effect. She never imagined that one of her colleagues would consider it selfish and unacceptable, a betrayal. "I wanted to go back to the work I love. There's no hidden nefarious anti-feminist scheme to it."

Dakota took another sip, making a sign to the waitress. "This is amazing," she told her. "Could you bring me another one?"

"Coming right up," the young woman promised.

To Rae, Dakota said, "Right. It sounds really silly when you put it like that, but I can promise you, that's not how I meant it. I worked hard to be where I am. I know you did too. Only to give it all up? I don't get it."

Rae, too, needed a bit more of the sweet boozy treat to get through this. Especially when she could easily remember a younger self that might have seen things the exact same way.

"You're right, we both worked damn hard. You know what I think? We've come to a point where we've earned the right to make decisions that benefit us, and our families. My life changed. I made a decision. It's not going to jinx your chances of going up the ranks. In fact. I'm pretty sure you will, regardless of what I decide to do."

Dakota was silent for several heartbeats.

"Other than that, why does it matter so much to you?"

Especially considering how connected the Lords were. Promotions were likely in Dakota's future. Rae's thoughts regarding this subject were without spite or illusions. This was simply reality, and at least Dakota was passionate about the job and good at it.

To her surprise, Dakota started laughing. Her cheeks were flushed, from alcohol or self-consciousness, it was hard to tell.

"Now here's something silly. You were kind of my idol."

"And I fell off my pedestal. Ouch."

"Part of it might have been less than rational," Dakota admitted.

When she received her second cocktail, Rae ordered a second one as well, ignoring Grace's grin.

"Yes and no. It's not like I haven't had these thoughts, but at some point, we have to do what's right for us, don't we? Otherwise, where does it stop? I wanted something safer, and a more regular schedule, when we had Simon, and I thought things would stay the same. But they didn't, and I know this is where I need to be. It's not just about the money."

"I get it. If it had been about that for me, I would have gone with one of my parents' career choices."

Rae detected a multitude of emotions in those few words. Frustration. Longing. A bit of regret perhaps.

"They put a lot of pressure on you?"

She assumed that might be the case when money and legacy were in the picture. Her parents never had bestowed that kind of expectation on her, and she and Genevieve couldn't imagine doing it to Simon.

"They had...preferences," Dakota said. "Me being a cop or queer wasn't one of them, but they adapted best they could."

For a few seconds, Rae was completely distracted from their conversation, for all the wrong reasons. That was none of her business either.

"I'm sorry," she offered.

"What? The word queer?"

"No, I don't have a problem with it. I was married to a woman. I just didn't know about you."

"Well, now you do."

Things were happening a lot faster than Rae had anticipated, and she needed a moment to process. So, she was Dakota's fallen feminist hero. What did that mean? Did she ever think...Did Rae? When in doubt, the answer was certainly another sip of the excellent house cocktail. She and Dakota were finally on the same page about something.

"Well, thanks for trusting me with that," she said. "I can assure you I didn't know Mark was going to assign me to the case until he did. I'm sorry if that made things more complicated for you, but I believe we've made some good progress."

"Since you came on board, yes."

"That was the plan, I imagine. A case like that, it's a lot."

Dakota stared darkly into her glass, her mood shifting. "No kidding. I've been to scenes that were much worse, but this one...I'm trying not to let it get to me. To think that he made them have dinner with him, and they knew they were going to die. Why does he hate them?"

Rae sensed that the question was mostly rhetorical, but she answered anyway. "Lots of reasons. They're more successful than he is. They're women. They rejected him once, or he imagined they did. If it's not any of the above, he might not think it's about hate. He might think he's doing them a favor."

"How?"

"I don't know. Sarah's father was violent, right? Do we know about anything similar in Marla's family?"

Dakota shook her head. "Nothing from her sister or her parents."

"Dolls and funny PJs. I wonder if there's a connection somewhere."

"You think he brought the PJs too, dressed them in them? Jesus, this is even more fucked up than I imagined."

Rae didn't disagree. "It is. I think we have to dig into the women's childhoods more. Chances are Sarah wasn't the first."

"You are so optimistic, Rae Burton."

"Just...experienced," she attempted to lighten the mood some.

She was unprepared for Dakota's smile, or what it did to her.

"So everyone keeps telling me..."

Rae avoided her gaze. One complication at a time.

The next morning, she could finally see her son's smiling face, making her forget about deranged possible serial killers and other challenges in her life.

"Love you, Mom," he said before he was off to join his friend who had arrived with his mother.

Gen came back on the screen after seeing them out.

"Hey. I'm glad we could make time."

"Me too."

Simon was happy in Paris. It was written all over his face. He seemed to love everything about his busy schedule. He loved Rae. He hadn't said he missed her, because probably he didn't have time. Rae couldn't help the pang of disappointment, and predictable subsequent guilt. She should be happy for him, no conditions, right?

"You two look good," she said. "Paris really becomes you."

Gen laughed. "Paris becomes everybody. Have you thought about what we said last time?"

Truth be told, Rae had thought about many things. Some days she felt like sitting by the door like Rex had for months, waiting for the two of them to come back.

But she had a new, exciting, and challenging life to live.

"Next vacation time, I could do a few days, I think. I promise I'll try."

"Please do. Simon would love it. He talks about you all the time."

Rae was torn between several responses, none of them appropriate. *Why wouldn't he? I'm his mother!* Or, *would you love it too?* Are you seeing anyone? Not that Gen owed her an answer to the latter. She was free to do whatever she wanted as long as it didn't impact Simon negatively, and from the looks of it, he was thriving.

"Like I said, I'll see what I can do. We're pretty busy right now."

"Yeah."

She could swear Genevieve was suppressing a shudder. Rae had made it a point not to bring work home. Her ex-wife had always been uncomfortable with the reality of her job, even when Rae spent most of it in an office. She couldn't hold back the yawn.

"You stayed up late last night?" Genevieve didn't have the same reservations. "Did you go out with your colleague again?"

63

Notice the singular.

"As a matter of fact, I did. We had some things to discuss."

"I see."

"No, you don't. Job-related things. Like murder."

"That's what's making you blush?"

"I'm not...Gen, I have to go. Give Simon a kiss from me and tell him I love him. Again. I'll see you."

After the screen went dark, Rae shook her head as if denying the charge. Her cheeks still felt warm. She hadn't told a lie, had she?

Chapter 9

Leaving the lieutenant's office, Dakota observed Rae's arrival with mixed feelings. She had a friendly word for everyone, and her environment clearly reacted to that. Dakota felt like she'd reacted to her a little too much last night, lowered her guard. She usually knew how to keep her distance, and it served her well, with colleagues and criminals alike.

The moment people found out that she was connected to *the* Lords, they treated her differently. She had received disdain, jealousy, and unjust privileges because of her family name, though she did her best not to take advantage of the latter. The line could be blurry sometimes.

Rae had made her furious, but last night, she had also made her comfortable, more than she had been around her before, anyway. The setting and the house cocktail had certainly played a role. Perhaps Dakota's problem was that she didn't know how to be comfortable. More than one ex-girlfriend had hinted at the possibility, and she was beginning to think there was some truth to it.

Speaking of which...

There was a reason why she had wanted to take care of those calls with the Bedford children quickly. Her conversation with the son had gone expected. She had met him on a few occasions. He and Mona had different groups of friends, so they had rarely spent time together.

Mona...What was she doing here?

"Hey, Lord," Baker called over from where she was standing next to his desk, wearing a visitor's badge. "There's someone here for you."

Rae looked up briefly but went back to whatever she was working on.

Bracing herself, Dakota forced a smile and went to greet Mona.

"Hi. I'm surprised to see you here."

Mona shrugged. "My parents had yours over for dinner yesterday. I guess I was feeling nostalgic."

So, this had nothing to do with Sarah Cooper. Dakota wasn't sure if she should be relieved or annoyed.

"It's nice to see you," she said. "But I'm afraid I have work to do, and I'm only here for a couple of hours this morning."

"Could you make time for lunch later?"

Dakota cast a quick look at Rae who had her gaze hefted on the screen.

"Look, you said to get back to you if there was anything else I remembered. I did. I don't know if it's important."

"Okay. Let's go somewhere private to talk. Would you like a coffee?"

"Ah. No. I think I'll get one later."

Dakota shook her head as she led Mona to the breakroom. Bad coffee in police stations was such a cliché. These days, they, too, had decent machines. The coffee was fine unless you compared it to the Viennese coffee house in the city center. But she was more curious about what Mona had to tell her, so she held back her thoughts.

"This is about Sarah?"

"I don't know anything about your other cases. You're still working on it, right?"

"I am," Dakota confirmed, starting to get antsy. That happened easily these days, and her and Mona Bedford in the same room did not help.

"Okay. Good. So yesterday at dinner, Tim mentioned that Sarah complained to him about a student at the university who was harassing her. Probably one of those woke people she was always raising money for."

"Tell me more," Dakota said, proud of herself for not cringing. There was a reason why she and Mona hadn't lasted long. In fact, their brief fling had been mostly desperation on Dakota's part, frustration when everything good in life took too long, and no one seemed to understand her. Now she did cringe. Yes, that was a long time ago. She had found her place.

Just like Rae had. She couldn't keep being mad at her for it, could she? Not when Rae had a good point: They had both earned the right to make their own decisions about their lives.

"Yeah, well, he didn't like where she was procuring donations from. Apparently, he had a list of names of all the," she made quotations with her fingers, "unacceptable people, which included us, and your folks. She laughed it off at the time, but..."

Dakota had trouble believing that someone unhappy with the way Sarah did her job would go to such lengths—then again, they had just lost their best lead.

"Tim didn't mention this to me when I called him. Why isn't he here?"

"You know Tim, he's busy. And he knows I have a good reason to check in with you, so—two birds, one stone."

"I guess. All right, can you give me a name?" She was still going to follow up with Tim. She was tired of these families, including her own, doing whatever they wanted, always treating their own time as more important than everyone else's.

"He didn't know him, and Sarah didn't give a name, so you'll have to check with the university. That's all I can tell you. I hope it helps."

"We'll look into it. Thank you, Mona."

"You're always welcome."

Her words seemed to imply more than this information. Dakota chose to ignore whatever else she might have meant.

"Thanks. I'll see you out."

Of course, Mona had to wait until they had an audience before she kissed Dakota goodbye. She'd always had a flair for drama.

Dakota hoped Rae hadn't noticed, but when she saw her smile, she realized she likely had.

Time to get out of here soon. She would drive by the university on the way home.

To her surprise, Tim Bedford was just leaving the campus when she arrived.

"Tim! Do you have a moment?"

He turned to her, the surprise evident in his expression. They might have talked on the phone a few days ago, but she had rarely spoken to him in person in recent years. When they were younger, they'd never paid much attention to one another. Mona had brought Dakota to his office a few times when they were still dating. Clearly, he was comfortable living the kind of life Dakota had left behind best she could.

"Dakota Lord. Hi. I thought Mona was coming to see you this morning."

"She did. I was going to follow up with you anyway, but since you're here...I was wondering why you didn't tell me about the guy harassing Sarah about the donations."

"I forgot about it," he said with a shrug. "I'm really sorry, but I didn't think it was important."

Two women dead, both of them harassed days before the murders. In his defense, he didn't know details about Marla's case, but still.

"Well, it might be. You don't know the guy's name?"

"No, and I'm sure Mona told you. I have to go, but let me know when you're free, and maybe we can get a coffee sometime if you want to talk more about Sarah?"

That wasn't how it worked, but the offer surprised her, so she let his words stand.

"You have more to tell me?"

"Maybe," he admitted, "though I don't know if it has any bearing on your case. I was trying to look out for her. I liked her."

"You two were dating?"

"No," he denied. "Friends. It's terrible how she died...Everyone is just moving on. I just came from a meeting with her replacement."

"I'm sorry. Sure, we can have a coffee sometime next week. Pencil me in?"

"I'll always make room for Mona's friends," he said with a smile.

"Good to know."

She headed to the dean's office but was stopped short by her assistant who told her that Dean Lowell had gone home for the day. The woman made no secret of the fact that she, too, was about to start her weekend.

"A few students have objected to those donations over time, but they still enjoy using the labs and equipment," she said.

"Anyone that stood out? Who might have gotten violent?"

"I don't know anything about that. Dean Lowell might, but you'll have to come back on Monday."

"Well, thank you for your time."

Great. She had a potential coffee date and another needle in a haystack. What a way to start the weekend.

Dakota had an idea. She was quite sure that it wasn't a good one, but what was life without a little risk?

Chapter 10

As much as Rae had tried and sometimes succeeded not to bring work home, especially on a weekend, she didn't always succeed.

It was a completely different lifestyle when you came home to a family demanding your attention. Rex might have been offended if she'd shared that thought with him, but to be fair, he didn't demand a lot of attention other than food, water and occasionally, affection, on his terms only.

That left a lot of time to ponder the case while she was doing a load of laundry and later, vacuuming. Perhaps she could go grocery shopping, cook something for a change...Rae had promised herself that she would be her own person, take care of herself, but the temptation of take-out was often too great. She hadn't taken that much of a pay cut.

"What are we going to do?" she asked Rex.

If he was a human, he would have shrugged and walked away. As a feline, he could only choose the latter option.

"Thanks buddy. I appreciate the help."

She put away the vacuum cleaner—Rex wasn't afraid, he just loudly complained—when the doorbell rang.

Rae wasn't expecting anyone which, in itself, was kind of sad. She had her own circle of friends, and some she had shared with Gen who didn't place the blame for the divorce on either one of them. She hadn't been that good at maintaining any of those friendships, she reflected. Her only dinner invitation in months had come from her boss.

She didn't realize she was still wearing the frown when she opened the door to an apologetic Dakota Lord.

"Oh, is this a bad moment? I'm sorry. I shouldn't have come unannounced."

If she hadn't, it would have given Rae a moment to comb through her hair and change into something nice, and why would she want to do that anyway?

Dakota had, though. This was the first time she saw her in a dress under the open coat, the hem ending a couple of inches above her knees. Realizing where her gaze had gone, Rae cleared her throat.

"No...This is fine. Come on in. I just finished some chores."

"I hear you," Dakota said with a sigh as she followed her inside. "I could never keep up before I hired my cleaning person."

Rae suppressed the smile, not sure if she had been successful. Dakota had a cleaning person. Of course. Her place was likely substantially bigger than Rae's too, not the usual on a detective's salary.

"Lucky you. So, what's up?" This was a surprise. She had imagined that after last night's conversation, they both could use some space. Rae had had her suspicions, but she never imagined Dakota felt this passionate about her decisions...about her. She had to stop it right there.

"And who do we have here?" Rex had joined them, meowing enthusiastically when Dakota dropped to her knees and petted him before Rae could utter a warning.

The traitor. He had taken longer to warm up to Rae, and that was after she became the only person to feed him.

"Meet my roommate Rex. A word of warning. If you ever have kids and they ask for a pet—it's a trap."

"He's beautiful."

Studying the scene in front of her, Dakota being this unusually open and relaxed as Rex snuggled against her leg, her throat went dry. This was strangely...domestic. Familiar. She couldn't have these emotions, the longing, realizing how much she had missed being with someone.

Obviously, she'd have to restrain herself because Dakota Lord wouldn't be that person. Not only were they still somewhat at odds about some things, but the woman who came to the station earlier had made no secret of where she stood with Dakota.

"Oh, I'm so sorry. I got sidetracked by your lovely roommate."

Dakota got to her feet, looking self-conscious all of a sudden.

"Don't worry. It happens. He's sneaky that way. So, what's going on?"

"If you have a minute?"

"Yes, of course."

Dakota took off her coat and hung it on the rack before she followed Rae into the living room.

"Please, sit."

Dakota chose a spot on the couch. "I spoke to Mona and Tim Bedford earlier." She shook her head. "We should have found out about this days ago, but they were *busy*." Her intonation told Rae what she thought about that explanation. "Anyway, they told me a student was harassing Sarah for donations she accepted from conservative donors. I'm not sure what he expected attending that university, but still. Neither Tim nor Mona could give me a name, but I found something."

She took out her phone and scrolled until she found the video of a small protest outside the university. It showed Sarah Cooper walking by, her shoulders hunched against the rain, or maybe the attendees' anger.

"Look at him."

One of them, a man in his early to mid-twenties, broke from the crowd and got in her face.

"Do you even know where these people invest their money, how many lives they wreck? Do you care?"

"If you want to file a complaint, please make an appointment."

"That's the problem, Ms. Cooper. You're not taking any appointments unless someone writes you a check. You're accepting blood money."

"Come on, Trevor. Show me some real proof, and we can talk about it."

The video ended, but Rae had seen enough for some renewed optimism.

"Trevor. If he's enrolled, it won't be so hard to find him. Both women were harassed before their death. That's not a coincidence."

"I don't think so either. What are the odds that he's another dead end? Even if he is and someone set him up, there has to be some connection."

"I agree. Good work."

"Thanks."

It was probably just Rae's ego imagining Dakota was the slightest bit flustered by her praise. Either way it was a nice thought, warming her...oh shut up.

"That was Mona Bedford this morning?" Careful.

Dakota looked surprised at her question. "Oh, yes. I'm sure the air was filled with a sense of past mistakes and regrets."

"Why?" You don't have to sound so happy about it. Besides, all Rae had seen was two attractive women who would naturally gravitate towards each other. Same age, same social class.

"In short? I hope Trevor didn't kill Sarah because I sympathize with his cause. Mona thinks he's a spoiled woke guy who needs to catch up to the real world. Which is…rich. You saw that purse. I know what it costs."

"I imagine she has a cleaning person too."

Her deadpan comment made Dakota laugh out loud, and Rae was ridiculously happy with the result.

"Believe me, she has help with lots of other things too. I was young and foolish. Let's not talk about this anymore."

"Fair enough," Rae acknowledged, though she might be a bit too sensitive about any age-related comment. "This is progress. Would you like a drink?"

Dakota's eyes widened slightly, though she smiled, as if welcoming the non-sequitur.

"What do you have?"

So, she had nothing better to do on a Friday night. Rae filed away that information for further reference. And, she and Mona Bedford were over a while ago. The day was starting to look up.

She looked at Rex who was curled up next to Dakota.

Thanks, buddy, she thought, and it wasn't sarcastic this time.

"How's a pinot grigio?" she asked.

"Perfect."

They were going to crack this case.

Chapter 11

For the second time in two days, she was drinking with Rae Burton. Dakota found that much of her irrational anger had evaporated, leaving her with a feeling of slight embarrassment and regret. She still thought she had somewhat of a point...She could have chosen to make it in a different way. Ask questions first. Didn't she take pride in distancing herself from the snap judgment so many people she'd grown up with, made?

Like Mona. How they'd ever be friends, let alone lovers, was a mystery to her, but she had to admit she wasn't immune to stereotypes. And projection.

"I'm really sorry," she said when Rae filled her glass again. Rex had taken a liking to her, curling up next to her, head on her leg. She petted him absent-mindedly.

At least Rae seemed to accept her apology easily.

"I get it," she said with a shrug. "I thought it was better to raise the subject in case it had an impact on the work. I think we've been making good progress nonetheless."

"On the case or in general?"

"Both. I'm glad we talked."

"Me too."

"Good. I don't know about you, but I could go for some food. I'm afraid I can't promise you a home-cooked meal, but if you were okay with ordering in...?"

Before Dakota could answer, the sound coming from Rae's phone indicated an incoming video call.

"Excuse me for a second."

"Of course."

"Hi," she could hear the cheery voice.

Rae frowned as she walked a few steps away. "It's late. Is everything okay?"

"We're fine, just having a late dinner party with friends. Simon is sleeping. I wanted to check in with you."

"I'm good. Thank you."

"Are you okay? You sound a bit stressed."

"I'm not, but I haven't had dinner, and...I have a guest."

Dakota wondered why Rae would lower her voice like that, until it sank in. Oh. The ex-wife. Another intriguing part about her new colleague, not that Dakota ever intended to get married. Too many people did it for the wrong reasons. She wasn't going to be one of them. To be on the safe side, it was best to avoid it altogether.

"Okay...You must tell me more soon. Have a good night. Simon wants to call tomorrow morning if that's all right."

"Of course. Thanks. Goodnight, Gen."

Rae kept her gaze on the screen for a couple of seconds before she looked up. "Sorry about that. So, how's Thai?"

Having Thai food with Rae, some more wine maybe, in her apartment that was both cozy and elegant sounded...tempting. They had laid it all on the table, and even though she might not be done apologizing and feeling awkward, this was a kind of comfort she hadn't enjoyed in a long time. The guys at work were fine, but she had established a certain image for when she was around them. They didn't question it, and she was okay with it. She could be one of the guys, and they didn't care what she paid for a pair of jeans.

Then, her other circle, the one she had distanced herself from, did care a lot. It could be lonely. And here she was with a gorgeous woman, comfortable on her couch with her cat, and a glass of wine.

Why would she want to be anywhere else?

What was she hoping for?

She looked up into Rae's warm eyes, realizing she'd never answered her question. If she wanted to impress the woman who had been her crush from afar, she had to do better. She should go.

"That would be great," she said instead. "I love Thai."

"Me too. Next week will be busy. Who knows when we have the time again?"

Her smile made Dakota's cheeks flush, the idea of again.

Dinner. Like a date. No, there was no way no-nonsense Burton had meant that, especially after Dakota had all but insulted her the other day.

"Good point. You have a menu?"

"So, we'll go back to the university and find Trevor," she said after the food had arrived, and they sat down again in the living room.

"Sounds like a plan. I'm still wondering if there's some sort of childhood connection. Not necessarily between Sarah and Marla, but something he saw in them that reminded him of past events, triggered..." Rae frowned. "I hate to use the word in this context."

"I know what you mean."

"Nevertheless, we know we're looking for explanations, not excuses. No sexual assault. He thinks of them as children?" The frustration was palpable in her voice. "I think it's about time to call in help. We need a real profile."

Dakota didn't disagree. She too had been puzzled by the set-up, and what it meant.

"Yeah. Let's go to the university early on Monday, hopefully bring in Trevor and talk to Castillo afterwards."

"We'll do that."

They fell silent. Despite the heavy subject matter, and their rocky start, it wasn't uncomfortable, just the opposite. Dakota found herself secretly studying her host and partner who was wearing a pensive expression as she held on to her glass. Even in comfy clothes, in her home, she had something elegant about her. She might have preferred to come back to detective work, but she still had that air...boss woman. Despite Dakota's mixed feelings about decisions that weren't her own, she was more intrigued than ever.

Running into Mona and being reminded of past mistakes hadn't made her more careful.

"Why did you get divorced?" she asked.

Rae's gaze held nothing but surprise.

"I'm sorry. I don't know why I said that. None of my business."

"That's okay. I wish I could give you a good answer. It sounds like a cliché, and maybe it was, but we drifted apart. In the end, we wanted too many different things."

"Career-wise?" Apparently, she couldn't help herself.

"Among other things, yes. I wanted to raise a family here, and I thought we were on the same page. We talked a lot about it before I took the lieutenant's job. We were about to buy a house...and then Gen gets a job opportunity and takes it and makes plans for Simon to live with her."

"That must have been tough."

Dakota already disliked the woman who had been on the phone earlier, though she admitted to herself that she might have ulterior motives. Perhaps part of her misplaced anger was at herself because it seemed like she hadn't overcome her crush after all.

It was complicated. To work with her, to maintain her own professional confidence, and not wonder...

"It was, at first, but you know what they say. It takes two. I might have neglected to mention how much I hated sitting in an office, telling people what to do, dealing with the politics of the game."

"You didn't tell her you were unhappy." She nearly apologized again. She thought she had an argument to present, but the more she learned about Rae, the more she realized the woman didn't do anything on a whim, let alone big life-changing decisions. Dakota's reaction had made her look childish.

"Not for a long time. You make compromises, right? We realized our visions of the future differed too much. I was angry at her at first, but Simon is thriving in Paris. I couldn't deny him that."

"Paris. Wow."

A small sexy smile curled Rae's lips.

"Don't tell me you've never been to Paris."

"I have been, a few times," Dakota admitted. "Not in the past seven, eight years though. I always thought I'd go back sometime...With the right person."

Too much wine. Too much pressure. Too much Rae.

"Gen keeps telling me I should come visit them. I should, for Simon, because I have no idea when they will be back. Not before Thanksgiving, in any case. To be honest, I think the romance aspect is overrated."

"No way," Dakota protested. "It's one of the most beautiful places in the world. I could show you."

"That would be a challenge."

Clearly, and the fact that Rae's ex and her son lived there didn't help. What was she thinking anyway? They had to work together. Rae had not shown any indication that she could be interested...Drinks the other day, that was because she wanted to clear the air. Wine and Thai food and introducing the cat happened because Dakota had invited herself...She wanted to shake her head. It was getting complicated.

"Maybe. I should go. Thank you for dinner."

"I didn't make it. And you paid your share."

"For the company, then. I'll see you Monday?"

"Sure," Rae said after she got up and followed Dakota to the door. "Are you okay?"

"Yes. It's just getting late."

To her relief, Rae didn't remind her of the jibe she'd made about going out on a school night. Childish. She had to lay it off.

"Okay. Have a good night."

"You too."

There was an awkward moment where she thought there might be a hug or something, and either one of them might initiate them. She heard Rex meowing as she fled the scene.

Chapter 12

Rae could have been irritated with Dakota for various reasons—she had resented her for things that were not up to her to decide, she had shown up unannounced and sort of hijacked Rae's evening, and she had asked nosy questions.

If all of that wasn't enough, she was late.

Early on Monday, Rae parked in front of the university's main administrative building, waiting for her, still contemplating Friday evening and its abrupt ending.

Would she ever figure her out? Some detective she was, so good at her job that she had left a better-paying position to get back to it.

She couldn't be angry at Dakota when it was clear they had so much in common. She had hoped to have all those questions figured out by now, but clearly, she had fallen short, and that wasn't her younger colleague's fault.

But Rae was far from being irritated with her. Dakota didn't remind her of missed opportunities. She had enjoyed the time they spent together, and perhaps she was afraid she had enjoyed it a little too much.

She willed away all those complicated musings when Dakota finally pulled up behind her. Time to get to work.

At this point, the dean was likely happy to get them out of her sight as quickly as possible, because she found them a name and an address in record time.

"Trevor Gaines, has had a couple of run-ins with campus police because of protests." She sighed. "He's here on a partial scholarship, apparently wants to be a rebel. He'd been badgering Sarah for a while."

"We'll look into that," Rae promised. "Thank you for your time."

The woman's wry smile told her she'd heard the implied "again."

Dakota hadn't spoken more than a few words, before and after the interview. Rae told herself not to read anything into it. They both had lives outside of work, and outside of that tentative rapport they had formed. It didn't have to mean anything.

They both took their own vehicles to the address the dean had given them, an apartment building close to the university where many students resided.

Trevor lived on the third floor, with a couple of roommates. They found his apartment door, and Rae knocked, tensing when she realized the door wasn't closed properly. It opened a few inches. She carefully pushed it open all the way, her hand going to her weapon as they both stepped inside.

"Trevor, are you there? We're with the police. We're coming in."

Loaded silence greeted them as they walked into the living room past a small kitchen. On the left, a short hallway gave view to two closed doors. There was another door to the right, across from the kitchen, half open, a bedroom visible behind it.

"This is bigger than I thought," Dakota said. There was a small noise coming from that bedroom.

Rae put her finger to her lips. She carefully stepped closer but before she could inspect the source of the sound, a black-clad figure emerged. At the sight of the gun, she reacted instinctively, tackling her partner to the ground as the bullet wheezed past them.

The man ran past them to the open window, not before firing another shot. Rae returned fire, but he was already outside and on the fire escape.

Glass rained down from the broken top part of the window.

"I'm fine! Go." Dakota struggled to her feet as Rae ran after the intruder—or Trevor? She only caught a glimpse of him as he headed down, jumped the last part, and ran, too far gone. As she was calling in the shooting, she hastened back to Dakota who stood, looking pale but otherwise okay.

"Wow. That was not the greeting I expected."

Rae reached out to touch her shoulder, fighting the impulse to draw her into an embrace.

In the living room area, one of the doors opened slowly, and she spun around, raising her weapon again.

"Please, don't shoot!" a terrified-looking Trevor Gaines, holding up his hands, implored. "Oh God, please tell me you're really the police."

Rae lowered her weapon and holstered it, looking from him to the shattered window and Dakota next to her.

"We are," she said. "Detective Burton, this is my colleague Detective Lord. We have a few questions for you. Let's take this to the station, shall we?"

He didn't object.

"Are you okay to drive?" she asked Dakota when they were standing outside the building. Rae had cursed herself for being caught off guard, but taking action usually helped her get back into a sense of normalcy.

"Yes, sure."

"Okay, I'll see you in a bit."

Dakota had been quiet after the incident, but she, too, went back to doing what needed to be done without missing a beat.

Trevor had left with a couple of uniformed officers and would be waiting for them at the station. Rae wished she could have given a better description of the intruder.

Alone in her car, she acknowledged how close of a call this had been. Maybe they were going at this wrong, still. Maybe someone wanted to distract them by all this serial killer lore, rituals, childhood connections, poison, and so on.

Who else could have an interest in killing two women and coming after...whoever Trevor Gaines was in this. A witness? They would soon find out.

They had to move forward, but she still made time for a coffee run. Rae knew at least two—make that three—people besides her who would appreciate it.

Mark Castillo joined her in the hallway on the way to the interrogation room.

"You mind telling me what happened there?"

"Of course not." His terse tone held more concern than criticism, she knew. "We learned that Trevor Gaines was openly criticizing, if not harassing Sarah Cooper for accepting donations from right-wing sources. We wanted to talk to him, but when we arrived there, the door was open. An intruder fired a shot, I fired back at him, he fled. Gaines had been hiding in his bedroom."

"And you make time to get coffee for everyone."

She wasn't quite sure what to make of that tone.

"One of them could be yours."

"Always efficient." He gave her a relieved smile. "I'm glad you two are okay."

"Thanks."

"I mean it. All that paperwork."

"You're funny. Take your coffee or leave it, I have a witness to interview."

Mark laughed. "Yes, Ma'am. Boss."

The banter relaxed her some, just in time. They arrived, and she opened the door to where Dakota was waiting in the observation area.

"Just one more thing," she said. "I didn't get a good look at him, but I gave a description. If we find that guy, we'll be a lot closer to solving those murders."

"I agree," Dakota said. "Oh, thanks. I love you," she added with regard to the coffee. Her favorite specialty, vanilla latte.

Rae always paid attention.

"I'm glad you get along so well," Mark said. "Now get me some answers."

Trevor Gaines jumped when they entered the room, but his eyes lit up when Rae sat the coffee in front of him.

Everyone could use something sweet today, and she planned on sweetening him up enough for him to tell them everything he knew.

"Mr. Gaines, thank you for helping us out." Unless he was the person they were looking for, and that looked less likely now, he was probably feeling safer here at the station.

"I'm not sure what I can help you with but..." He swallowed. "Anyway. What do you want to know?"

"You had a few tense conversations with Sarah Cooper."

Dakota remained standing, sipping her coffee. She looked her usual sweet self, but her expression left no doubt she was serious.

"Sarah. Yes. It's such a shame what happened. She was brilliant."

"Yet you had serious disagreements," Rae reminded him.

"Well, sure, but..." His eyes widened. "You didn't think I...Sarah and I were friends!"

"We have a couple of witnesses that tell a different story. That you harassed her about some of the donations she got for the university."

"What? No." Either he was a good actor, or that disbelief was real.

"Unfortunately, yes. Do you always get in your friend's faces like this?"

Dakota walked over to the table and held up her phone for Gaines to see the video of the heated exchange between him and Sarah.

Gaines wasn't impressed.

"But she knew I was with the group, and I can assure you she agreed with me. Do you really think Sarah was happy having to deal with all those rich, spoiled people? The stories she told me sometimes...She said the only thing making the job worthwhile was that the money would go to many good causes. But some of them outright wanted to buy their own curriculum."

"Did she give you names?"

He shrugged. "The usual suspects, like the Bedfords, the Lords, and the likes of them."

Rae noticed Dakota's frown. She wondered if he had forgotten how she had introduced Dakota, or if he simply didn't make the connection. She realized her colleague still looked pale.

"Okay. Do you know if she ever felt threatened by anyone?"

"More like annoyed. I don't think those people would kill anyone. They just threaten to take your job, but Sarah was always polite, didn't tell them what she really thought of them."

"How about you?"

"What do you mean?" he asked, obviously taken aback by Dakota's icy tone.

"You're not always that polite. Is it possible that you got in someone else's face? Let something slip that Sarah told you in confidence?"

"No!" He shook his head. "Why would you say that? I don't engage with those types, and for sure I wouldn't betray Sarah's trust. I'm only telling you because she's dead, and you seem to think I had something to do with it!"

Rae cast a look at Dakota, but she didn't continue her line of questioning.

"Let's move on to today. Do you have any idea who came to your apartment?"

"If I had, I would have told you already. But you saw the video. I assume a lot of people did, so perhaps someone wanted to shut me up. What?" he asked in Dakota's direction.

Rae, too, was curious about that non-committal sound.

"Protests on campus, one way or another, are a common thing," Dakota said. "I can't remember any gunshots being exchanged in recent years. Are you sure it's not something else?"

"I don't do drugs if you wanted to hint at that. I don't know. Who gave you my name anyway?"

"That's not important. What exactly happened this morning?"

Tim Bedford, Rae remembered. Brother to Mona, Dakota's ex. Family friends of the Lords. It couldn't be easy.

"I heard someone trying to break in. So, I hid in the bedroom, and I wanted to call the police, but I had forgotten my phone...I didn't see him, like, at all, but I heard him walking around, opening cabinets and drawers. I was hoping he'd think I wasn't home and leave. That's when you came in."

Rae shared a look with Dakota who wasn't hiding her frustration. They were still going around in circles.

"Have you ever heard of Marla Peters?" she asked.

She hadn't expected him to start crying.

Chapter 13

As a little girl, Dakota had once fallen off a horse. Literally. And true to the saying, she'd gotten back on it, stubborn and unwilling to admit she'd been scared.

But at that point, she had enough experience to push through the scary moment.

She had no time for the trip down memory lane or ponder any similarities to the present situation.

Trevor Gaines knew more than he had told them.

"I can't believe they're both dead!" He was nearly sobbing now.

"How did you know Marla?" Rae asked softly.

"We were in a couple of classes together," he said. "She took evening classes, but she managed to attend two during the day. We talked sometimes."

"Were you friends with her too?"

Dakota's sharp tone made both Rae and Gaines look at her. She saw no reason to take it back. For now, he presented a connection between the two victims.

"Not like with Sarah, but we were...friendly if you will. I guess you know already that she was suffering from PTSD. Crappy family. It wasn't the same for me, but I got jumped on my way home once, and someone threatened me with a knife. I could relate somewhat."

"When you say family, you mean?"

"Come to think of it, similar to Sarah, though the abuse was more emotional. Marla used to get locked in the basement for punishment."

Was he for real? If he cared about either woman, why had he never come forward? The behavior of witnesses could be mind-boggling.

"Why are you looking at me like that? It was never my story to tell. Besides, Sarah's father and both of Marla's parents are dead now. None of this is important to your case."

"With all due respect, Trevor, let us be the judge of that. Would you like another coffee?"

He stared back at Rae in confusion. "Is this really important?"

"It might be. We'll likely be here a bit longer. My colleague and I will be right back, so, can we bring you one?"

He shrugged. "All right then. I can't imagine how this helps, but if you want, I'll tell you what I know."

"Thanks. We appreciate it."

"Oh my God, how are you not losing your patience with him?"

The look Rae gave her told Dakota that her reaction might have been a tad over the top. Who could blame her? It wasn't Trevor's fault, but she got shot at today. That could make a person a bit cranky. Come to think of it, given how much he had kept from them, she wasn't yet sure about him.

Then again, Rae had also been there, and she appeared as calm as ever. It made Dakota wonder if she'd been in this kind of situation more often.

"It's becoming a bit of a challenge," Rae admitted. "But what's important is that he's given us something. There is a connection between Sarah and Marla. I think the hair, the PJs, all of that is related to some sort of childhood fantasy the perp wants to create."

"Something real? Something made up?"

"Unfortunately, we have no idea yet. It's almost like he wants them to be safe in a twisted way."

"By poisoning them." She shook her head, hoping Rae knew that the sarcasm was not directed at her. Not this time. "I know what you mean though. He probably knew about the abuse. Twisted doesn't even begin to cover it. So, what is your impression of him?"

She looked back to the window. They could see Gaines leaning forward. He looked pensive though not extremely worried. Good acting or a lack of guilt?

"Perhaps he and Sarah were really the kind of friends that agree to disagree. Marla...It could be a coincidence. Maybe it's not, but I doubt he would arrange the situation we walked into."

That was a diplomatic way to say it. She couldn't suppress the shudder.

"Everything okay?"

Rae laid a hand on her shoulder, the touch warm, both comforting and confusion. She couldn't deal with this now.

"Let's get that coffee and wrap this up, okay?"

Rae didn't argue, and they went to the breakroom to get three cups. Dakota eyed the vending machine and decided against any other purchase. She would treat herself properly later.

Prompted by more coffee and the fear they might still consider him a suspect, Trevor shared what he knew about Sarah and Marla's families. They had heard about Sarah's abusive, now deceased, father. There was no reason to believe he hadn't died of natural causes.

To Dakota, locking a child in a basement sounded barbaric, and also, like something that could be related to the murderer's M.O.

"Did she ever describe to you what the basement looked like?"

He shook his head. "No, she understandably didn't want to go into details about that. She still had a fear of the dark."

"Did she mention any dolls?"

"I don't think she was allowed to have any toys when her parents locked her in."

Children's PJs and braids. At that time, Marla was the age where she might have worn those.

Dakota and Rae tried every angle, but Gaines' knowledge obviously had its limits. He, too, was shaken by today's events. When her gaze met Rae's, they both knew that they wouldn't get anything else out of him.

"Can I go now?" he asked.

"Yes. Thank you, Mr. Gaines. We'll be in touch. In the meantime, if you can remember anything else..."

"Sure." He accepted Rae's card, on his feet a moment later. "I'll be staying with a friend. I can text you his address if you like."

"That would be helpful."

This time, even Rae's tone held a trace of sarcasm. Dakota suppressed a smile.

They saw him out, and from there, went straight to brief the lieutenant on their progress.

She was happy to let Rae do most of the talking, though even Rae's calm and professional delivery couldn't hide the fact that they had a lot of dead ends, and few viable leads to follow up on.

She thought of the victims, the connection Trevor had given them. The gunshot shattering the window, the scenery around her vanishing in a brief flash of anger before she was able to pay attention again.

The women had overcome their childhood trauma and enjoyed successful careers.

Somewhere along the way, someone made them the target of their sick fantasies...but what exactly was the fantasy? Why did he think it was up to him to protect them? Random? Something in his own biography?

After the meeting she went back to her desk, pulling the files for both women again, opening her own notes on them and what little they had on the perpetrator.

Rae hovered close, and Dakota wondered if she was still worried, the thought filling her with irrational resentment. Highly irrational because the woman had saved her life. She was grateful above all.

She didn't want to think about it any longer, and the recent developments should be enough to keep her mind occupied otherwise.

"Okay, hear me out for a second. If that's really the connection, and he wants to 'protect' them in this creepy way, what if there was someone in his family whom he wanted to protect but couldn't? His mother maybe."

Rae looked intrigued but still doubtful.

"I hear you, but what's the next step? How do we narrow down the cases? If the abuse was ever reported, that is."

Dakota wasn't finished yet. She appreciated being distracted from the memory of ending up on the floor, narrowly escaping the bullet. So much.

"That depends. I think he's their age, a few years give or take. The age his mother was when he was little. The case might have made the papers. There could have been a murder."

"That's a lot of ifs."

"Think about it this way. We didn't know what connected Marla and Sarah beyond the university, but you're right, the fact that Trevor knew them might have been coincidence. Marla had a couple of classes during the day, so there are bound to be others who knew both of them. It leads back to the university."

"Yeah. It's worth looking into. You want to get started on this?"

"Sure."

"I can drive you home later if you want."

Now, she was more obvious about it.

"I'm fine," Dakota stressed.

"It's no problem. I can pick you up in the morning."

She didn't need pampering, that, Dakota was fairly sure of. But perhaps part of her was willing to play with fire.

"All right, then," she relented. "If you want, we could have dinner at my place."

Rae seemed both surprised and pleased at the invitation.

"I'd have to check on Rex first if you don't mind stopping by my place first?"

"Of course. Now let's find our perp."

Despite all her bravado, Dakota couldn't help the relief knowing she wouldn't spend the evening alone. She wasn't scared or worried that the shooter might come at them a second time.

Regardless, this had been too close.

Chapter 14

It wasn't Rae's intention to ignore what had happened. She knew this would be impossible, but she preferred to focus on the immediate. No one got hurt, not severely anyway. Getting tackled to the floor, Dakota might feel a bit sore, but that definitely beat getting shot. The small scratch caused by a shard from the exploding window hadn't stopped Rae.

They were fine. Trevor Gaines, the shooter's primary target, was fine.

That was all that mattered for now.

They had even managed to unearth a few cases that might fit into Dakota's theory.

All in all, a successful day.

Still, her throat went tight for a few seconds when she scooped up Rex. He didn't resist, probably sensed her state of mind.

"Okay, you have fresh water, food, and litter. You can handle a few more hours, right?"

She had the feeling that he'd be rolling his eyes at her a lot if he could.

"I love you too. I'll be home soon."

She had tried Gen and Simon, but only reached Gen's voicemail with her cheery message. That would have to do for now.

Dakota was playing it cool. It was Rae's responsibility as the senior partner to make sure she'd be okay, right?

And dinner was the perfect setting for that. She glanced at her standing in the doorway, expecting her to perhaps make a joke about people who talked to cats, but instead Dakota's gaze was affectionate. Maybe more than that. Whatever it was, given today's events, it wasn't the time for it.

"Okay. I think he'll be fine for a few hours. Let's go?"

When they pulled up in front of the building that housed Dakota's apartment, Rae couldn't hide her surprise. She had driven past the historical building many times, and she remembered when it was being restored. She had read in the paper about the restrictions contractors had to observe. Rae had been more than financially comfortable for the past few years, but this was something else.

She was aware of Dakota's gaze on her as they walked into the tastefully furnished and decorated lobby.

"I'm not judging," she clarified. "It's beautiful."

"It is, and you wouldn't be the first. I don't know if that makes it better or worse, but I inherited from my Grandma, and my parents taught me how to invest early."

"Seems you've done well for yourself. So, you're not raiding the trust fund yet."

Dakota gave her an alarmed gaze. "I would never..." She shook her head with a laugh when she realized Rae had made a joke. "Okay, you got me. I try to balance my frivolous privileged spending with some responsibility. My parents haven't disowned me yet, but they aren't too fond of some of the organizations I support."

"Family can be complicated," Rae amended.

"Yeah. Look at the case. Lots of complicated family histories there."

They had reached the elevator and rode up to the 12th floor. Not the top floor, Rae noted. Yet, when they stepped into the spacious apartment, she nearly gasped.

Dakota's wardrobe at work was inconspicuous, business attire. To Rae's trained eye it looked expensive, though she didn't think Nathan Baker or their other male colleagues noticed or cared. The luxury in Dakota's home was tasteful, but obvious in every corner, including the view.

"Speaking of beautiful," she said, turning to her. Rae lost her train of thought for a second. It had to be the unexpected danger they'd faced together, or else she would have to acknowledge there might be something else between the lines. She meant the surroundings.

She meant Dakota as well, no matter how complicated things had between them from the beginning. And if she admitted what was really on her mind, it would be Rae making things infinitely more complicated.

"I'm glad you think so. Now, let's make dinner."

"Make?" For some inexplicable reason, her voice had gone up a notch. Dakota laughed.

"Yes, sure. When I need to clear my mind, I cook. That's why I always keep a stocked fridge. Come on."

"All right."

In the chef's kitchen that looked like it had been installed yesterday, all shiny surfaces, Dakota opened fridge and pantry and took out ingredients.

"Can I help you with anything?"

"Do you trust me?"

"I do." Tonight, her voice did all kinds of strange things. She had to get a grip. Senior detective, making sure her partner was okay after a close call. Right.

"Good." Dakota motioned for her to sit at the island, then put two glasses and a bottle of wine on the countertop. "You won't regret it. Something else I got from Grandma, I'm a pretty good cook. She always said that money isn't an excuse."

"Good for you." Rae found herself smiling, starting to relax. "I don't know that we had that kind of conversations in our house."

"Few people do. That makes it even more important not to be an asshole with money."

"You think anyone on that donor list is?"

Dakota took her time to answer, but to Rae's relief, she didn't seem offended.

"You mean Mona? She doesn't question any of it, but that's nothing out of the ordinary. She and Tim are both vying for the top spot in the family business. There's nothing much else on their minds, I guess."

Rae took a sip of her wine, remembering the parents, and the statements the siblings had made.

"You know the people on the donor list better than anyone of us. Do you think there's been any abuse in the past?"

From the stove, Dakota turned to her with a doubtful gaze. "I don't think Mona's going around poisoning people. On that list...Yes, I know most of them, and I know that abuse happens in every social sphere. I'm not aware of anyone in particular though. You're still thinking about that list?"

"Let's cross-reference it with the old cases we found, see if anything comes up."

"Yes, we'll do that. But now I'd like to focus on making my guest happy."

The abrupt turn of the conversation and all the possible implications almost made her choke on her wine. She, too, needed a bit of distraction, if not from the events of the day.

Dakota hadn't promised too much. She even served dessert, a delicious chocolate raspberry cake that tasted boozy, and coffee from the expensive brand machine.

"You made this yourself?"

Dakota laughed at her puzzled question. "I also bake when I get stressed, and this case has been stressing me out a lot."

"Everything was amazing. Thank you so much."

For a heartbeat, Dakota's smile seemed strained. "Well, it's the least I can do. If it wasn't for you, I might be in the hospital tonight. Or worse." She shook her head. "I don't know what's up with me lately. I didn't see it coming at all."

"Neither did I. We went to see a student, remember? With everything we have on the perp, even if Trevor had been him...We wouldn't have expected a shooter."

"Maybe."

"No, not maybe. This wasn't your fault or mine. We weren't careless."

Abruptly, Dakota turned to get the coffeepot from the counter and refill their cups.

"A bit more cake?"

"My eyes say yes, but I might regret it."

"What are you talking about?" Dakota's eyes unabashedly raked over her body. "You look amazing."

"Thank you." Could a woman her age blame her blushing on a hot flash at least? The room felt pretty hot all of a sudden. "It's not what I meant though. I gave up the guilt a decade ago, but I really don't have any more room."

"Okay then. I can give you some to take home later."

"That would be great. Thanks. And I meant what I said. Mark was worried, and of course he has reason, but not because we did anything wrong."

"I get it. Let's just...not talk about it for five minutes, okay?"

"No problem. How about I help you clean this up before I go? Rex is probably starting to get cranky."

"My housekeeper will do it tomorrow. Could we just sit for a moment?"

"Yes. Of course."

Despite her request, Dakota barely stayed a couple of minutes after they sat down in the living room. "Excuse me."

Rae nodded and sat back to admire the stunning views once more, though her mind wandered back to the scene earlier today. So much could have gone wrong. She still believed they couldn't have anticipated an active shooter given that the murderer they were looking for had his preferred ritual. But what if he wanted to tie up loose ends? What if the shooter wasn't related to their case at all?

They had gotten the tip about Gaines from Tim Bedford, Mona's brother. They kept coming back to that family.

She got up, deciding it was time to check on her colleague. She deserved privacy in her own home, but she had also gone through a traumatic experience. Rae could remember nights she'd spent alone before Gen and Simon in her life. Sometimes she had found it hard to make sense of the reality she was confronted with on the job, but as one of the few women in the precinct, she couldn't let it show. Rae hoped that things were different for Dakota's generation. To some extent, it was up to her to make it so.

She knocked softly on the door of the bathroom.

"Come in."

Dakota stood in front of the large mirror, her eyes rimmed with red. She shook her head.

"This is embarrassing. The last thing I had on my mind."

"Don't worry about it. You were nothing but professional today. This is your home. You can—"

Rae's words and good intentions were cut off abruptly when Dakota stepped into her personal space and kissed her. Despite the less than perfect situation she couldn't help enjoying the thrill of soft lips on hers, the excitement of something this unlikely turning real. It felt familiar, maybe because she had thought about this, and dismissed the idea again. The kiss wasn't a tentative ask for permission either.

They indulged themselves in the moment until Dakota stepped back, her face flushed. Rae had a hard time reading her expression, but she was quite certain self-consciousness, maybe regret, could be in the future.

"I'm sorry," Dakota said. "I didn't mean..."

Of course she didn't.

"I should go. Are you going to be okay?"

That was the whole point, wasn't it?

"I'm fine."

"Okay. Good night."

Talk about complicated. This was not what she had expected to happen in the first couple of weeks on the new job. But Rae had to admit it was the best thing that had happened so far, no matter how much more awkward it would make their work together. A no-win situation.

She should get on that dating site already because there was no way Dakota Lord would want to pursue this any further once she was over the events of the day.

Chapter 15

Morning came too soon. Dakota had to muster every bit of responsibility not to call in sick. She still felt sore from having been tackled to the floor, if for a good reason.

She hadn't meant to hide in the bathroom to cry, or for Rae to come after her.

Everything had gone so well, the rest of the day, the evening they'd spent together—it wasn't fair that in a heartbeat, she couldn't seem to breathe, her thoughts revolving about the moment that could have ended so differently.

She didn't want to ruin the evening, until she had.

Way to go, Dakota. Good luck trying to convince Rae you're not a spoiled trust-fund brat. Her cooking skills might be decent, but likely not enough to make up for everything that happened afterwards.

You still want me to pick you up? Rae texted.

No, thanks. I'll walk.

With a sigh, she finished brushing her hair and left the bathroom, picked up her keys and exited the apartment.

From her apartment building, it was a twenty-minute walk to the station, which should be enough time to clear her thoughts.

The problem was, maybe she didn't want to apologize for something that had felt this good. Better than anything in a while. She might have been more in shock over the day's events than she could admit to Ray and everyone at work, to herself, but she did remember.

Rae had kissed her back, and for a split-second or so Dakota had indulged the fantasy of a different outcome.

She felt safe with her. Last night, she needed safe.

This wasn't Rae's fault though. For one, she wasn't the type to take advantage of the situation. Would she have been interested under different circumstances?

Probably not. She was friendlier than Dakota deserved given their rocky start, but she was also accomplished and experienced on a level that Dakota had yet to reach. Why would she be interested?

Why had she kissed her back?

She was getting annoyed with herself, pining for that woman like a teenager. They still had a job to do. Determined, she walked through the sliding doors and waved hello to the officer at the front desk before she took the elevator to her floor.

Rae was, predictably, already sitting at her desk. The memory of last night was too vivid. What had she been thinking?

"Detectives, a word?" Mark Castillo, who had just arrived, motioned for both of them to come with him.

Rae gave her a smile as they followed him, whispering, "Hi. How are you?"

Dakota shrugged and winced.

Inside the lieutenant's office, she said, "We found a number of cases—"

"There has got to be a connection to the perp's childhood." Rae spoke at the same time.

"I see you're making progress, but one at a time please."

"Both Sarah and Marla came from abusive families," Dakota started again, at the same time as Rae said, "We are looking into a possible connection—" and then stopped. "With the donor families," she finally finished.

Castillo's expression was somewhere between surprised and irritated, but he didn't mention their less than stellar communication.

"You continue with that. Hang on," he added when his phone rang.

Dakota cast a quick sideways glance at Rae who was now studying her feet. Would she ever stop creating situations for herself that required her to apologize?

The lieutenant's serious tone told her that neither of them would have much time to dwell on that kiss or whatever it meant. He ended the call a few seconds later.

"A witness reported an abduction a few minutes ago. The woman's name is Cindy Loman."

"Fuck," Dakota heard Rae mutter under her breath, and she couldn't agree more.

"Cindy Loman, that's the woman who saw Damian Hodge threaten Marla."

"Where are we on him anyway?"

"He went to work, and home afterwards," Dakota said. "There was no indication that he was doing anything illegal, so we had to call off surveillance."

"Well, it looks like it's on again," the lieutenant said grimly. "Loman was taken right in front of the coffee shop before her shift started. Let Baker give you a hand and then bring Hodge in."

"Yes sir," Rae answered.

"You mind if I drive?" Rae asked softly when they walked down the stairs and headed to the parking lot.

Unlike yesterday, being in a car with her seemed too close, too much this time. After that kiss. Dakota had no time to worry about her feelings. She couldn't believe this was happening. Truth be told she had given up on the idea that Hodge was their killer, but they had him yelling at Marla and Cindy on tape.

He might have been under surveillance, but he had the right to go to the coffee shop, and if he hadn't caused any more trouble, he might have slipped under the radar. Until today.

"No, it's fine," she lied.

Rae pulled out of the parking lot, focusing on driving. The silence was close to painful. From the beginning, it felt like the perp had always been one step ahead. It was almost like he knew her, the way she worked, maybe her weaknesses.

He probably knew about her parents too, but few people in town didn't.

Cue the connection to the university's donors. Mona.

The car stopped, and she nearly removed her seatbelt until she realized Rae had only stopped at a red light.

Dakota almost expected her to ask whether they should talk about it. It seemed like a Rae thing to do.

Instead, she said, "If he took her, he's going down. We'll get to him first. He won't have time to go through with it."

It was hard to feel hopeful about anything regarding this case, but at least the thought distracted her from the elephant in the room.

Hodge expressed his outrage and threatened a lawsuit, but he went with the uniformed officers eventually.

Rae watched them get into the squad car.

"All right, that part is done. Let's just check something."

Dakota followed her back into the building. The man behind the counter looked flabbergasted at the turn of events.

"I swear I don't know anything," he told them unprompted.

"Just one question," Rae said, her warm tone putting him at ease immediately.

Dakota suppressed a sigh.

"Have you noticed anything different about Mr. Hodge lately? Has he been leaving work sooner than usual, coming in later?"

"Funny you should mention that," he said. "He came in just a few minutes before you, said his car was stolen. I don't know if he reported it already."

"Thank you. That's very helpful."

"He's not in trouble, right? I know he talks a big game, but he's no criminal..."

"It will be fine," Rae assured him. "Thank you."

"His car was stolen," Dakota said, shaking her head when they were on their way back to the precinct. "Oldest excuse in the book. He can't be that stupid?"

"Well, good for us if he is. Let's see what he has to tell us."

Before starting the interrogation, they went to a different room where Baker was talking to Cindy's colleague, a fellow barista by the name of Britney.

She could give a fairly precise description of the car and the driver. They had arrived at the parking lot of the mall at the same time. Cindy was walking to the door when a dark blue sedan pulled up to her, the driver asking her a question. When she leaned in, he pulled her inside and left with screeching tires. The man wore sunglasses and a non-descript black baseball cap, but Dakota hoped that footage from the nearby traffic cameras might yield a license plate.

"Everything went so fast," she sobbed. "You're going to find her, right? I wish I could have helped her, but by the time I realized what was going on, it was already too late."

Dakota refrained from telling her that, likely, someone had been planning this abduction. There was nothing she could have done to prevent it. She caught Rae's pensive glance.

"You called the police right away. You did the right thing," Dakota assured the young woman.

She knew words would only go so far after the traumatic experience of seeing her colleague taken. But they had something important to do now. With a little luck, this could be over soon, and they'd find Cindy alive.

Castillo joined them outside the room.

"Any progress?" he asked curtly.

"Witness gave a description, and they're also looking at the camera footage. We're going in with Hodge now. Apparently, he came in late to work today, said his car was stolen. We'll see what's up with that."

"All right."

Dakota realized that he didn't go back to his office, but instead followed them into the observation area. She wasn't sure if she liked the idea of her boss watching today of all days, but she understood that a lot depended on the outcome. They could save a life if they did this right.

She cast a glance at Rae, who nodded to her, and went inside first.

Hodge looked up at them, a wry smile on his face.

"I should have known this wasn't over. You can't talk to a woman anymore these days without you people getting your panties in a twist."

Dakota wouldn't waste any time asking him what exactly he meant by people, women, cops, or all of the above.

"Talking and threatening, two different things, buddy." She knew that suspects often underestimated her, and that made them let their guard down, but this was different. They knew each other already, no need to pretend.

He scoffed at the term but didn't respond otherwise.

"We're not here because of that incident though. We heard that you were late for work today. What were you doing this morning?"

Hodge rolled his eyes at her. "Like you don't already know. When I went to the parking lot this morning, my car was stolen. I still had to get to work, so I took the bus. I was late."

"You didn't think of reporting the theft to the police?"

"I was going to do it later, okay? I didn't want to miss work."

She glanced at Rae who shrugged.

"Okay. Your car is a dark blue sedan?"

"That's right. I'm sure you knew that too."

She didn't like that he was so assured, comfortable. Dakota laid a notepad and pen in front of him. "Could you write down the license plate, please?"

He complied.

"What the hell is this about? Not only are you making me miss more work, I get the feeling that you won't be working all that hard on finding my car."

"Oh, believe me, we really want to find that car, especially since it was used in an abduction."

"What?"

She could have used "likely" to be more precise, but the effect was a bit more dramatic this way.

"What the hell is this? I didn't kill or abduct anyone."

"You remember Cindy Loman?"

He looked at the photo, shrugged. "The chick from the coffee shop who threatened to call the cops on me. I only went back a time or two, and it was always someone else serving me. I had no desire to talk to her ever again."

"Because you were mad at her? Like you were mad at Marla?"

Rae's quiet question cut like a knife.

"You are insane! Are you trying to pin something on me? My car was stolen! Whoever did this, it wasn't me. I couldn't care less about them. I moved on!"

"Okay. I assume you can tell us which bus route you took. There will be witnesses, video..."

"You can bet your ass there will be. Can I go now?"

Dakota sat down across from him.

"We will check all of that, but maybe there's another way you can help us."

He stared back at her sullenly, conveying that he wasn't much interested in helping. No surprise.

"Could you think of anyone who might have an interest in putting a spotlight on you? Someone you had a fight with, who threatened you?"

Hodge's gaze turned calculating, as if he was trying to gauge whether he could trust them with whatever information he had.

"I don't get into fights," he said. "Find my car, would you? Can I go now?"

Masking her frustration with a smile, Dakota told him, "Of course. Just don't leave town until we've confirmed your alibi, please."

"I can't go anywhere. No car, remember?"

Chapter 16

Rae hadn't missed the way Dakota avoided her gaze. She couldn't blame her. After all, Rae had done nothing to make the situation less awkward, first by kissing her back, then by running out on her.

How could she have been this careless? She knew that a high adrenaline situation like the one they'd shared stirred up many emotions, made people let their guards down. When what had seemed a safe but unrealistic fantasy all of a sudden became true, she went with it. In the light of day, it was clear to her that she owed Dakota an apology—or an explanation. All of it would have to wait because a woman's life was on the line.

She was starting to think they were dealing with two different perpetrators, unless the killer had meant to cleverly set up Gaines and Hodge as well.

When Dakota hung up the phone, her frustration palpable, Rae knew that Hodge's alibi was confirmed.

"Got on the bus at his stop, didn't leave it until forty-five minutes later," she said. "There's no way he could have abducted Cindy...unless the bus driver was in on it. They have video too."

"Just great. We're starting over."

Rae almost regretted her words when Dakota's face fell.

"I didn't mean..." Probably she was just tired. They had been dealing with lots of new developments in the past few days. "How about you continue with the traffic cams, and I go over those old cases one more time?"

Dakota had no objections, or maybe she just wanted to make distance between them.

Rae went back to the files.

Needle in a haystack. No kidding. They had found a few where violent abuse in a family had erupted into murder, but nothing yet to tie the case firmly to the recent killings. Rae shuddered at the descriptions, cops trying to put unspeakable horror into words. Children kept in basements, sometimes for days without food. For punishment, because of neglect, and so on.

A name caught her eye, and she decided it was as good a start as any. The case had happened before her time in that precinct, but she'd spent a few years working with the detective in question.

Carla Savino was now retired, but she might remember.

Rae caught her at the airport.

"Rae Burton, of course I remember you! How are you? Aren't you a lieutenant now? Good for you."

On the way to a beach vacation, she sounded cheerier than Rae had felt in over a year. Except maybe while kissing Dakota Lord...No. She couldn't think about this now.

"Thanks. Look, I won't bother you for long, but I have one of your case files here. Two kids locked in a basement by their parents, you remember that?"

To her relief, Carla didn't try to deepen the subject of Rae's career, and Rae didn't see the point in correcting her right now.

"Unfortunately, you'll have to be a little more specific. I dealt with a few fucked up families." Her tone was calm and matter-of-fact, though the anger came through clearly.

Rae wanted to cringe at her choice of words but found it appropriate at the same time.

"Father was abusive, tried to kill the mother? A boy and a girl were found in the basement, the girl unresponsive."

"Oh, that one. Rae, I'm about to board the plane, but I'll send you an email before we take off. I often wondered what became of those kids. Just quickly…That was a terrible situation. And yes, he tried to kill his wife, but get this, he had been gone for a few days when the police came in."

"I read that." She had read it twice. The timeline seemed strangely off.

"The woman was so traumatized, she wasn't able to take care of herself or her children. They were in the basement left to their own devices."

"Jesus."

"Yes. When we went in, the brother was holding his sister in his arms. She was unconscious but made it. At first, we thought it was because of the lack of food and water, but then we found out she ingested some kind of poison. Probably an accident because they were hungry. Rae, they're calling my flight."

"Okay. Thank you so much. One more thing—I find nothing about the boy, did you test his blood too?"

"Geez, I don't remember," Carla said. "They put a rush on the girl's tests because of her condition. I'm sure they checked that he was okay in the hospital. I'm sorry. I have to go."

That was already more than she had expected. Rae stared at the report in front of her, wondering if they had the right family. This particular horror story might turn out to be their lucky break.

Martin Kinsley was ten years old, his sister six. According to the report, both had been exposed to abuse and neglect, likely for years. Could those experiences turn someone into a killer? It was possible. Those children would harbor a lot of anger against the adults in their lives but were unable to express it without severe repercussions.

Some kind of poison.

It might still be an accident, and whoever was committing these crimes had added this specific memory as a detail. She thought of the victims, Sarah and Marla. Abusive families. Poisoned, dead in a basement in their own home. Too many similarities to be coincidences. Her bet was on the brother, simply because of statistics, but what if the sister was the one who had taken up the killing? Because she hated the helpless girl she'd been? Because she wanted to end her suffering?

It was hard to tell at this point, but Rae was certain that finding Hannah and Martin Kinsley would help them solve this case.

She looked over to Dakota's empty desk. She'd update her later—preferably with addresses for the siblings. If this worked out, and she was starting to feel confident about the possibility, they might not have to call in any exterior help, like a profiler. Castillo would appreciate it.

Half an hour later, Dakota still hadn't returned. Rae's search had led to mixed results and moderate success: The case of the two siblings had attracted a fair amount of press. The headline *Flowers in the Basement* made her cringe, but she read on until other shocking events took over. Martin and Hannah had both gone into foster care. Hannah had a locked social media profile, but it wasn't too hard for Rae to figure out that she lived in a small town about two hours away.

Martin's whereabouts remained a mystery. They would talk to Hannah and go from there.

Rae picked up the phone and called. She waited four, five rings, but no voicemail came on. When she was about to give up, the phone was answered, and a hesitant voice asked,

"Hello?"

"Am I speaking to Hannah Kinsley?"

"Who is this?" Her voice sounded firmer now, and suspicious.

"Detective Rae Burton, Homicide. I was hoping you could answer some questions regarding your family."

"My family?"

"Your parents—and Martin."

"They're not my family." The scathing tone made Rae flinch. "I don't want to talk about them. He was a fucking abusive drunk, she didn't do anything, and my brother fucking tried to kill me. You wouldn't want a family like that, would you?" Gone was the air of intimidation and fear. It was clear—and not surprising—that Hannah Kinsley was still grappling with those traumatic childhood experiences.

"Hannah, please, don't hang up. First of all, I'm so sorry this happened to you."

"Yeah, many people have told me that. It didn't happen to me though. It was done to me."

"Yes. You're right. I apologize. What did you mean when you said your brother tried to kill you?"

"I meant what I said. He put poison in my food, something he found in the basement. He said we needed to be quiet not to upset Dad...guess what, the asshole was long gone."

"I don't understand."

"He was gone! Our mother didn't do anything, when he was around, and after he had left. So, Martin went upstairs to get us something to eat, cereal, applesauce, whatever he could find. He must have put the poison into it. They said it was an accident, but I don't believe them. He knew our father was gone, yet he kept saying we needed to stay downstairs."

"Hannah, do you remember any dolls you had with you?"

She laughed bitterly.

"Oh my God, those dolls. They sure were ugly, but they were all I had. I used to sit them in the window, so they could look outside...and I might have hoped that someone would see them and realize we needed help, but that never happened."

"Again, I'm sorry. Could you tell me where your brother is now?"

"I'm happy not to know. I heard he was adopted. They didn't bother trying to find a family that would take both of us, which was a good thing. Maybe they realized I was scared as hell to be under the same roof as him again."

If all of that was true, how could he have stayed under the radar this long? And how long had he been killing?

They'd have to take a hard look at motive again.

"Has he ever tried to contact you?"

"No. I think he knows that I'll call the police the moment he does."

"Hannah, thank you so much for talking to me. We might have some further questions..." They definitely would, but now Dakota was standing in front of her desk, gesturing to her. She was wearing her Kevlar. "Hannah, I have to go. I'll call you."

"I guess I can't avoid it, Detective Burton."

"Dakota, I have something—"

"It will have to wait. Someone saw a man bringing Cindy into his apartment. She was out of it. They described the sedan as well."

"All right. I'll tell you my side of the story on the way."

Dakota looked thoughtful but didn't comment.

"Will you be all right?" Rae asked when they headed to her car. She almost expected Dakota to dismiss her question, but instead, Dakota returned, "I have to be."

They definitely had to talk—again—hopefully after arresting Cindy's kidnapper.

Chapter 17

D akota could feel her heart pound, and it wasn't because of Rae sitting in the car next to her. In fact, in the light of day and the demands of their job, that strange, exciting moment seemed far away.

The job, not so much. She had to get a grip. What were the odds of getting shot at twice in two days?

Pretty good, actually. They were likely about to come face to face with a man who had abducted a woman in broad daylight. Chances were he wouldn't ask questions first. But they were prepared, she told herself as they arrived in front of the building. The tactical team was getting in position. She could feel herself starting to sweat under her Kevlar. There was nothing new or unexpected about this situation, so why couldn't she seem to take a deep breath?

Rae was still watching her, but she didn't say anything.

Dakota appreciated it. "Let's go," she said. "Let's get her home."

"Yep. That's the plan."

Despite her promise, Rae didn't have a lot of time to share her findings, but what she had told Dakota made her think that today would be a long day.

They approached the six-unit building, three apartments on each side. The address they were going for was on the right, ground floor. Rae's expression was now one of tense concentration, and Dakota acknowledged that she had to focus as well if she didn't want to repeat a highly unpleasant experience.

The team in front of them breached the entrance, and she and Rae followed suit into the apartment.

It was sparsely furnished as if someone had just moved in, no sounds to be heard as they went through room after room.

A wooden staircase leading down to a basement was next. When they entered the narrow dark hallway, Dakota clenched her left hand into a fist hard enough for her fingernails to dig into her palm, the sensation centering her.

Seconds later, the tension vanished into thin air as it was clear the kidnapper was gone.

Cindy Loman, tied to a chair in the middle of the room, duct tape over her mouth, stared back at them through wide eyes, though she didn't seem physically harmed.

Dakota could breathe again.

She let Rae do the comforting thing while she took a look around. A window at ground level. A room furnished with a single bed, a table and a chair the same kind Cindy had been tied to, and an empty bookcase. No knickknack or books, no dolls on the window. Had they prevented another killing?

Either way, this was a win. She forced the emotion aside, signaling Rae who was still talking softly to Cindy that she was going to make the usual calls. A CSU would go over the place with a fine-toothed comb, hopefully finding matching DNA, and more.

After Cindy had been checked out at the hospital, they'd see what they could learn from her, and then decide what to do about Hannah, who might be the killer's sister.

She cast another glance at Rae, grateful for her presence.

⟡

"I have to get home. I need to feed my cat."

Cindy, now in an exam room at the hospital, still seemed a tad confused and scared, which was understandable after the day she'd had.

"I understand," Rae said softly. "I have an Abyssinian named Rex waiting at home, and he gets very annoyed if his bowl isn't filled at the right time. The doctor will let you know when the results for your blood test are in, and you can probably go home after that." She paused for the young woman to process that information. "Cindy, I know you've had one hell of a day, so let's do this as quickly as possible. You arrived at the parking lot of the mall..."

"He asked me about opening hours," Cindy said, shuddering. "I just leaned a little closer, and he grabbed me. I was so afraid."

"Did you recognize him?"

"No, I'd never seen him before. I'm sure it wasn't the guy who yelled at the woman the other week. Was it the killer? You still haven't found him?"

"Not yet. Cindy, do you remember anything else? A tattoo maybe, a smell?"

"I'm so sorry. No. Wait. He had this very intense aftershave, one I thought only older guys used."

Rae looked thoughtful at that. Even Dakota thought that older was probably a relative term coming from Cindy, but she asked anyway,

"You have any idea about the brand, or what kind of scent?"

Cindy shook her head. "I'm sorry."

"That's okay. Is there anyone you can stay with tonight? An officer can drive you." Rae picked up the thread.

"I'll call my sister," she said. "Thank you for finding me."

She burst into tears, and Rae didn't hesitate for a second but folded her into a quick embrace.

"You were very brave," she said. "Take good care of yourself. We'll be in touch."

Dakota managed a smile she hoped was encouraging, though she felt beyond drained as they walked to the elevators. That, and she wanted those arms around her too. When had it come to that?

Burton had gone from an almost unattainable Idol to fallen hero to the woman she couldn't stop thinking about. If she was honest, that had happened before the kiss.

During the drive, her thoughts were meandering between the memory and the vague information they'd gotten from Cindy.

"You want to take a break, or...?" Rae ventured when they had arrived back at the station.

"No. We still have a lot of work to do. Let's grab a coffee on the way, check in with Baker, and then you can tell me more about that Kinsley family."

"Okay." They picked up their beverages, Rae a black coffee, Dakota spontaneously opting for a hot chocolate. Rae didn't comment, but Dakota hadn't missed the small smile.

"Hey," Baker greeted them, getting up from behind his desk when they walked in. "I found the building's owner. He's out of the country at the moment but get this: He says the apartment has been empty for months."

"That's interesting," Rae commented. "Thanks."

"You're welcome. I emailed you everything."

His cell phone rang, and he walked outside to take the call.

"So, Hannah Kinsley. She claims he hasn't contacted her at all," Rae explained when she was back behind her desk, comfortably leaning back into her chair.

Dakota noticed that her clothes still looked as crisp as they had at the beginning of the day. She might not have Dakota's wealth, but elegance sure came to her easily.

"Do you believe her?"

"I feel like I don't have the full picture yet. Obviously, Cindy's case was more pressing. We'll have to wait for the lab, and I thought in the meantime, we could pay Hannah a visit."

"That's quite the road trip."

This morning, she had been reluctant to get into a car with Rae, now the prospect seemed...intriguing. She was getting ahead of herself. It was about time that they solved this case, and she could go back to normal. Whatever that looked like, because Rae was here to stay.

"You got something better to do?" Rae asked, the corners of her mouth turning into a smile, her tone definitely suggestive.

Dakota could feel her face heat. She was a grown woman, damn it. She should act like it, even if Rae Burton chose an inappropriate moment to be flirty at work.

"Can't think of anything," she said. "Okay. Let's do it. I'd like to meet Hannah as well."

"It all fits." Rae was back to being all business. "The poison, the dolls...We have to find the brother, and then figure out the whole story, but I think we're on the right track."

"So, you don't think it's a rich people conspiracy anymore?"

"I never said it was. Let's see what we can find out from Hannah. I don't think we have to go there so early tomorrow.

We could come here, check in with the lab, and leave before noon?"

"Sounds like an idea. You'll give her a call?"

"No," Rae said. "I prefer the element of surprise."

They'd be outside their jurisdiction, and they didn't even know for sure if this was the right family. Rae's confidence was intoxicating though.

Finally, this story was coming to an end.

After that...Who knew?

"You are full of surprises, Rae Burton," Dakota said.

Rae's gaze told her she was taking the statement exactly as intended.

Chapter 18

Dakota yawned as she stood on the sidewalk, waiting for Rae to arrive. As they had discussed, they'd make a stop at the station and then head over to Oak Valley where Hannah Kinsley had found refuge after her ordeal.

Rae seemed to think that the story could still go either way, that both brother and sister might have a motive. It would be odd, Dakota thought, but very little wasn't about the case. Women could do horrible things...Still, most serial killers were men, and the presence of dolls and cute PJs didn't change the fact that two women were dead.

When they arrived, the lab was still working on the evidence gathered at the house where Cindy Loman was held, so they decided to leave right away.

"We will probably be back mid-afternoon," Rae assured Castillo after they'd informed him about their plans.

"An impromptu road trip," he said. "All right. Have fun."

That was a little out of character for his sober personality, and it made Dakota wonder about any possible hidden meaning.

He and Rae had been partners for years, and he usually had a keen eye when it came to his team's issues. Had he picked up on something?

Dakota couldn't help frowning. She hoped it wasn't the case. She was in over her head already, first acting like a brat around Rae, then...She hadn't quite figured out her mixed emotions, but that kiss remained on her mind. She couldn't help it.

"Speaking of fun," Rae said when they were on the road. She shook her head, and when she spoke, her tone lacked the sensual quality it had only a heartbeat ago. Or perhaps Dakota had imagined it.

"Yes?"

"What was that all about? It makes sense to go and see Hannah. I want to get a sense of her, her family, and if she really doesn't know where her brother is. I think all of this is better done in person—and it would be a lot to ask her to come all the way here."

"I agree."

"So?"

"So, what?" Dakota still didn't understand.

"You've been working with him for a while now. Don't you think that was strange?"

Maybe it was. Maybe Rae was just overly sensitive assuming Castillo might think of this trip as something other than a strictly professional activity. Then again, Dakota had assumed the same.

"I don't know. You were partners, I think you know him better than I do. It was probably just a throwaway line. He has a lot on his mind, obviously."

"Yeah, he's not the only one." Rae sighed. "I sacrificed breakfast time to speak to my son and ex-wife. I'm sorry, but I think if I don't get some caffeine and something to eat, I won't get anything done today."

"We can make a quick stop."

Talk about mixed, confusing emotions. It might be the high adrenaline from the past couple of days that left her with little sleep and dangerous ideas, but Dakota found even her partner's crankiness oddly endearing.

After all it was Rae who had suggested the early trip.

They found a diner on the side of the road where Rae ordered a full breakfast while Dakota succumbed to temptation and had a piece of lemon merengue pie with her coffee.

"I'm sorry, but I needed this." Rae closed her eyes after the first sip of coffee, her expression pure bliss.

Sitting across from her, Dakota could feel her face heat. She would have to be careful. Focus. They were here for the sole reason to advance the case. Everything else could, would have to wait.

Did Rae have sleepless nights too? What kept her up? Well, except for the case, and a family in a different time zone.

"The lab will call as soon as they have something, and if it's urgent, Baker will take care of it. Other than that...We can always stay a little longer today."

"Like every other day," Rae said grimly. "Something has to shake loose. I know Hannah can tell us more than she did on the phone."

"We did put in a lot of hours," Dakota acknowledged. "You seem very sure about this woman. I mean, I read the file, and I agree, it all fits..."

"There are a few pieces missing. Like Martin Kinsley. Where did he go after foster care? If he really tried to poison his sister, what was the whole point of it—did he for some twisted reason blame her for their situation? Wanted to protect her? We need to find him, and I think Hannah is our best bet for that."

"You're not going to use her to draw him out?"

Rae's gaze, a bit surprised and offended at the same time, told her what she thought of that suggestion. "No, I'm not. It's not our job to endanger civilian's lives."

"Sorry," Dakota mumbled, appropriately chastised. She knew she shouldn't have said it, though she couldn't help thinking that the chastising was kind of...hot. Maybe she had a fever. Should have taken a day or two after the shooting. "I know it's not," she added after taking a bite of her cake.

"I want to find out more about their relationship."

"Flowers in the basement."

Rae cringed. "I wasn't thinking about that. But as the older brother, was he protective, or mean? If he tried to kill her, and now moved on to ritualistic murder, what happened in between? I'm worried he might already know where she is."

"If she was worried about that, she might have moved further away," Dakota mused.

"You see, there are a lot of questions left. And I hope we can answer most of them today."

Dakota clinked her coffee cup again Rae's.

"I'll drink to that."

Rae gave her one of those long pensive looks, and this time, she held her gaze. The day might bring answers in more ways than one, the prospect exciting her.

They found Hannah Kinsley at work, a shoe store on the town's Main Street.

Her face fell when Rae introduced them, not a surprise. She looked around, but there was only one customer in the store examining a pair of high heels. Another employee was at the other end, stocking a shelf with new arrivals.

"You wasted your time coming all the way here?" she asked as if she couldn't believe it.

She wasn't thrilled, Dakota noticed, but not as nervous as she had expected. Hannah probably knew that she couldn't escape the past, and her biological family, forever.

She could relate somewhat, if not to the trauma Hannah had endured.

"I don't believe it's a waste of time. It would be really helpful if you talked to us."

Rae's tone was gentle but firm. For a second or so, Dakota thought Hannah might bolt, but she simply shrugged.

"I can probably take an early lunch break. Let me ask my co-worker."

The other woman had finished unpacking the boxes. They couldn't hear the conversation from where they were standing by the counter, but Hannah returned a moment later and picked up her purse.

"There's a diner next door," she said. "Let's go."

"Thank you." Rae gave her an encouraging smile which she barely returned, and they headed over to the diner where the lunch crowd had started to come in. They found a booth by the window. Rae let Dakota slip into the booth first before she sat, and Hannah took a seat across from them.

More coffee. The smells around them made Dakota inexplicably hungry—or perhaps cake for breakfast hadn't been the best idea. She forced herself to focus on the woman sitting across from them. Her light blonde hair and blue eyes were oddly familiar, even though Dakota knew she had never met her.

"I don't know what else to tell you," Hannah said with a shrug. "Our father was a mean drunk. At first, it was Mom who brought us down to the basement so we wouldn't disturb him, then Martin would take me. It got worse over time, and it seemed like Mom forgot about us more and more. We'd stay there for days at a time, couldn't go out, or to school…I have no idea how they got away with it. And then Martin snapped, too, and fed me that poison."

"I'm so sorry," Dakota told her. "I know this is hard, but your brother might be a person of interest in one of our cases."

"Might be? I don't think you'd come all the way here for a hunch. What did he do?"

"Someone has poisoned two women. The circumstances are similar to what you described on the phone, and what I could learn about your case," Rae explained. "Aside from the situation you told me about, was Martin ever violent toward you?"

Dakota held her breath, but Hannah Kinsley shook her head.

"No, never, that's why this was so much out of the blue. He always tried to cheer me up when I was sad, and he made up games, and stories about the great things we were going to do when we grew up and were out of that fucking house."

Either this was true, or Kinsley had suppressed a lot of childhood memories. Dakota wondered how someone could develop the mind of a killer when there weren't any signs before. She still thought Hannah looked familiar. It was driving her crazy.

"You both made it out," Rae said. "You mentioned you were scared of being under the same roof with him again."

"You bet. I was so sick! I thought I was going to die. I wouldn't trust him again."

"And you have no idea where he could be now? You didn't move very far away. Do you think he might still be in the area?"

"I can't say. But he often used to talk about how he was going to be rich. That was his go-to story, being adopted by a wealthy family, run a big business."

"And you? What was your dream?" Rae asked softly.

Hannah stared into her coffee.

"I just wanted the noise to stop," she said.

After Hannah had left, they sat in silence for a few moments. Hannah needed to get back to her shift but had offered to meet them at her home later.

Dakota could only imagine what their colleagues would think about her and Rae spending the entire day up here, but at the moment, she couldn't care less.

She was angry at the people never held responsible for what happened to the siblings, sad for the latter, but at the same time, cautiously excited. If they found Martin Kinsley, they might have the killer.

"She seems pretty open about telling the story," she said. "Do you still think she's withholding something?"

Rae's answer was a shrug. "I'd have to be a therapist to know," she guessed. "It's hard to say how they dealt with all of this in the aftermath, but she's not the one in hiding. She has a job, a home, seems fairly well adjusted. I know I had a different theory for a while, but my money is back on Martin."

"Yeah. If only we could find him."

Dakota had briefly talked to Baker who was going to try to trace Martin Kinsley's steps after the foster home.

"You seemed a bit startled when Hannah first came in," Rae observed.

So, she had paid close attention, not only to their witness. Dakota could feel her face heat for all the wrong reasons.

"I don't know...She seemed familiar. I can't put my finger on it."

Rae looked thoughtful. "Maybe you saw her picture in the case file? An article?"

"No, that's not it. Something about her..."

"Keep going," Rae suggested. "Maybe there's something there."

"I don't know. Maybe I'm just tired. It's about time this came to an end. What about you?"

"I'm good," Rae said with a smile. "All that coffee helped."

"Good. So now we...?"

"Wait. What else is new?"

Chapter 19

Rae didn't enjoy having to bring up traumatic memories for Hannah Kinsley, though she hoped that she could think of something during the day that would help them find her brother Martin.

Baker had gotten back to them. According to his findings, Martin's adoption records had been sealed, and he was in the process of obtaining a warrant for them.

Rae and Dakota were once again sitting across from Hannah, this time in her apartment where light and gentle colors dominated. It wasn't big, but the wall décor and arrangement of furniture gave the impression of more space. She had a huge photograph of a beach scene on one wall.

"Earlier, you asked me about my dream," she said. "I wanted to get far away from that basement. As you can see, I only made it to Oak Valley and the hardware store where they sell these posters."

"You have a nice home," Rae complimented her. She wished there was a way to put her more at ease, but with the subject matter of their conversation, that was an illusion.

"Well, thanks, but I'd prefer if we wrapped this up soon. Look, I know you were thinking I might come up with something, but I've spent most of my life trying to forget about my biological family, and that includes Martin. He wanted to make it big, have lots of money. At the time, it seemed nice to imagine, that he could protect us from our parents...but I guess he wanted it all for himself."

Rae couldn't help thinking that the ten-year-old boy had been only slightly older than Simon, the comparison made her shudder. She wasn't naïve about the world. She and Genevieve were doing everything they could to raise a child who knew he was loved above all, who understood that respect and kindness counted, and was prepared for the daily challenges of life.

Being confronted with how some parents just didn't give a damn or tried to mold their children into some extremist ideology never failed to infuriate her. Because all children started out innocent.

"Our colleague found out that his adoption records were sealed. Do you have any idea why?"

"No clue. Perhaps he did find his rich family, and they didn't want their names associated with that mess."

Rae had the same thought. She hoped that they wouldn't run into a brick wall of high-priced lawyers fighting the release of those documents.

"Is there anything else you remember?"

"If I did, I'd tell you, but I hope you find him."

"What else did you play with?"

Dakota's question seemed to come out of nowhere, but Rae soon had an idea.

"What do you mean?" Hannah sounded irritated.

"We talked about the dolls. Was there anything else? Something that was related to Martin's dreams of wealth, maybe?"

"Like I told Detective Burton on the phone, the dolls were all I had. Martin had a few toys, too, nothing extraordinary...but there was this piece of glass he kept with him, I don't know, I think it came from some broken figurine. He was always going on about having a huge airy office, with lots of expensive art. I remember he talked about it so much I got bored sometimes, but..." She sighed. "I couldn't say anything, because life upstairs was much worse, right?"

"Thank you, Hannah. Again, I'm sorry we had to bother you."

"Like I said...If you find him, it's all worth it."

By the time they left the apartment, it was dark outside. Rae checked her cell phone, and Dakota did the same. The last they'd heard from Baker was that he was going home and would continue tomorrow.

"We should go home too," Dakota said.

"Yeah."

"You don't sound convinced."

"I'm not. Something still doesn't fit. I'd like to call my neighbor to check on Rex, and tomorrow morning before we go, I'd like to coordinate with the local department and see if we can get a warrant for her phone records. Whether she's aware or not, I'm sure he has tried to contact her."

"We're not going to get a warrant on a hunch."

"No. I just think we could find out more if we stayed a bit longer and coordinated with the local authorities."

"Stay where?"

Rae hadn't missed that Dakota's voice had gone up a notch.

"Somewhere around here. I saw vacancies in a hotel, and there's a restaurant right there. I think we can make that work. I'm going to call Mark too."

Dakota's gaze was somewhere between apprehensive and intrigued. Rae assumed it wasn't because she was going to call Mark's private number.

"The sooner we solve this the better, right? That's what you said."

"Yes. I think—"

Rae waited, but Dakota didn't finish her sentence.

"What? You had plans?"

"No, not really. It's a good idea."

Despite her earlier surprise, Dakota seemed at ease when they sat down in the small pub where Rae jotted down notes on a notepad. She pushed them aside when the server came to their table.

"I think I'll have a beer," she said. "You?"

"That means we're officially off the clock?" There was something in her gaze Rae couldn't decipher. Amusement, interest...maybe she didn't want to look any further, because it would complicate things too much, or maybe she was afraid it wasn't everything she hoped it could be. Irrational either way.

"We are."

"In that case I'll have one too." Dakota named her chosen brand, and Rae went with the same. They each had a dish from the evening special. The waitress took both their menus and returned with their drinks a few minutes later.

When she had left, Dakota took a first sip, sighing in bliss before she leaned back in her booth.

Rae couldn't take any of it out of context, could she? What was the context anyway?

"I'm sorry if I made things weird," Dakota said, holding her gaze. "That wasn't my intention."

"I know. It was one hell of a day." After a pause, Rae asked, "What was your intention?"

"Like you said, one hell of a day. I wasn't thinking all that much, but I'm grateful that you were there. Thank you."

"You're welcome."

See? Nothing going on here. But her imagination had gotten so far ahead of her, Rae almost felt guilty for making them stay overnight. A cold shower might be in order. She was relieved when their food arrived, and they had something else to focus on.

Then again, why not? And if there was any chance, what could be a better occasion than this?

Talk about an angel and a devil on her shoulder. But they had come here for a reason, to locate Martin Kinsley. No distractions, right?

Chapter 20

Everything Rae had said made sense. There was nothing else to find here in Oak Valley. Regarding the case.

Apparently, what they couldn't find in town either were two single rooms.

"I'm so sorry," the woman at the counter said. "We have the fair this weekend, lots of exhibitions and guests from outside the state even. I have exactly one queen left."

"That's not your fault," Rae said reasonably. "We didn't know we were going to stay the night. All right, we'll take it."

Dakota wanted to laugh though she was worried it might send the wrong message. Caught in a romance trope with her partner. She hadn't expected that.

"You're okay with that?"

"Yes, of course."

The relieved clerk gave them the keys, and a form to fill. Dakota barely managed to hide her surprise, wondering how many establishments with such ancient processes even still existed. Rae, unfazed, filled out the information, and they headed upstairs to their room on the second floor. It wasn't huge, but clean and welcoming enough, with a TV, a desk and a chair, a small sitting area, and the aforementioned queen bed.

Dakota stood and studied it for a moment, wondering when she had last been so self-conscious about going forward...Maybe it was because she'd never kissed any of her partners after a life-threatening situation. They had all been men before. She'd never known anyone like Rae either, but there was an opportunity now. The realization felt kind of breathtaking.

"What did Castillo say?" she asked.

Rae turned to her, looking surprised.

"You called him earlier, right? What did he say?"

"Well...He agreed that it makes sense to coordinate with the locals in case Kinsley decides to show his face. Not much else. He was already home."

"If only we could see those adoption records."

"Yeah. That would help," Rae agreed calmly.

Dakota thought about how much she admired her calmness, in any situation really. She took control of her life, didn't care about what anyone thought. Dakota had access to enough wealth to live comfortably for the rest of hers, and the same would be true for a generation or two after her if they didn't waste it.

Yet, the questions never ended, if she was doing enough, on the job, with that privilege she'd been given...If she was enough. For anyone.

For Rae.

As if reading her mind, Rae stepped closer. Dakota held her breath when she raised a hand and brought it to Dakota's cheek, leaning in to kiss her gently. Calm. It wasn't like the hurried stolen kiss from the other day, the now-or-never feel after a dangerous situation. Maybe she hadn't completely distanced herself from it, but being here, in another town, helped. Had that been on Rae's mind too?

She wasn't going to question any of it. No one was going to run this time—convenient that they had nowhere else to go.

"I didn't realize you..." She let her words trail off, unsure how to phrase her thoughts. A warm shiver wound its way down her spine when Rae's fingers tangled in her hair.

Rae laughed softly.

"I swear, I didn't plan any of this. I wanted to follow up with Hannah, and I still believe it's important we don't overlook anything here. But...yes. I'm sorry I disappointed you. And I promise you I have been thinking about this since before the life-or-death situation."

"Before? When?"

Rae held her gaze for a long moment before she answered. "It was hard not thinking about it once you said you had a crush on me."

Dakota could feel the smile spread on her face.

"Well, I still do. And forget about disappointing me. I'm thrilled right now that you're not my boss."

"Are you? Why?"

Dakota thought it was better to show her with another kiss rather than tell her, and when Rae's hands wandered under her shirt, she knew she had gotten the message across.

She had assumed she might take a few days off after that case, take a vacation even. It had never occurred to Dakota that she could stop, even for a moment, while the investigation was still ongoing. Of course, unlike Rae, she never had to juggle the job with her family life and let go of the darker elements of humanity to help her child with homework or make breakfast for three.

But at this moment, here with Rae after a series of coincidences, Dakota realized what a relief it could be to leave it all aside for a few hours. Off the clock, it hadn't felt real in a while.

It did when she was in Rae's arms, their bodies entwined. So much for the trope. They hadn't cared to pretend any longer, brush against each other at night by accident. She could finally satisfy that fantasy, be with the woman who had intrigued and fascinated her from day done. The way Rae was touching her was nothing if not deliberate, taking her on a steady climb.

Her hands were warm, soft, confident as they learned Dakota's body. Giving up control wasn't something that came to her easily, considering she'd set out having to prove so much, to her family, her colleagues, most of all, to herself.

She had carried what some might have called a chip on her shoulder into relationships, with women who didn't care to call her bluff. None of it mattered at this moment.

She closed her eyes as Rae's lips touched her neck, and focused on the sensations, fingertips alternately caressing and arousing. She had been attracted to older, more experienced women before, but reluctant to follow through. There was a first time for everything. Dakota bit her lip, then gave up all pretense and stopped trying to hold in the moan.

Rae's arms came around her, and for the first time in a while, she felt like things might actually turn out okay, for both of them.

Chapter 21

B reakfast. Drop by the sheriff's office and see how they could best proceed in the search for Martin Kinsley. Head home, check in on a likely pissed Rex. Go to the station, update Mark, speak to the lab and hopefully make some progress.

As Rae stood in front of the bathroom mirror, going over the day in her head, she couldn't help smiling. She felt amazing, body and mind, the way she hadn't in a long time before the first coffee.

After her divorce, she had taken all the important steps. Therapy for a while, to make sure she and Gen had a good path forward as parents, to clearly voice her emotion, to reassess her career goals.

It was a long list already, and even though the therapist had mentioned it, and Gen did too, dating hadn't been on it. Rae had made good points: She'd be busy with the parenting from afar, taking care of Rex, and the job part. She hadn't shared it, but she had missed the easy camaraderie with her colleagues before her promotion.

Apparently, those had all been excuses—then again, she and Dakota weren't dating. Working under pressure, they had given in to convenient mutual attraction. But if that was all it would ever be, Rae had no regrets.

Even now, her face heated remembering Dakota's admiring gaze, the desire in her eyes before she leaned in for a taste. Somewhere in her forties, Rae had given up chasing everyone's approval, stopped caring what everyone thought about her choices and life, and that had proven to be a blessing. If she was honest, she cared a little what Dakota thought, and such admiration from a younger woman didn't hurt at all.

So, what if she had a bit of an ego about it?

A knock on the door jolted her out of her pleasant musings.

"I don't mean to disturb you, but I'm really hungry. I'll have you know I can get cranky if I don't get breakfast."

She opened the door to Dakota who was wearing yesterday's T-shirt with her panties.

"Then we don't want that to happen. I'm done. You can go in."

Too tempted by the sight, Rae changed her mind and pulled her close for a kiss, and she somehow ended up with her back against the wall. If either of them had any doubts how this would play out in the light of day, there was no need. The temperature in the room seemed to have jumped by several degrees.

"On the other hand, we might have a bit of time before that happens," Dakota whispered.

Rae wasn't going to stop her.

"This is the first time in weeks that I've spent a few hours not thinking about the job," Dakota confessed as they sat over a generous breakfast. Rae had chosen the pancakes with fruit, Dakota eggs with bacon.

"I'm glad. But...Don't do that. You're going to burn yourself out. I've seen it happen many times. Hell, I've been there."

"I know. I've been careful, but this is different."

There was a hint of warning to her tone, and Rae realized that she should probably limit the pep talk, given the circumstances. She knew, however, that Mark thought, and expected great things of Dakota. If she could help her in any way, she would. Well. Not just in that way, though Rae couldn't deny it had helped her too.

"I understand. I really do. This kind of case, it takes a toll. No one should be casual about it."

"I think you made the right call." Dakota took a sip of her coffee before she continued. "Coming here, talking to Hannah. There's something going on that we don't know about yet, whether she's a willing participant or not. She could be in danger."

"I was worried about that too," Rae admitted. "I doubt that we can get protection approved with what we have, but it's a small town. Maybe they can have an officer drive by her house and check in on her every once in a while."

"So, after this, we'll go to the station and have a talk with them."

"That's the plan. I hope they're interested in keeping in touch. We can go back after that, except I need to stop at home for Rex."

"Yes, of course."

Dakota seemed pensive, though Rae wasn't sure what occupied her attention. She waited a few heartbeats before she asked, "Is everything okay?"

"Just thinking."

That didn't tell her much.

"Like you told me last night, it's a good thing I'm not your boss." Rae tried to keep her tone light. "Everything else doesn't have to be complicated."

"I guess you're right."

There was a whole lot more behind those few words, but Rae was more than willing to take it slow, see where this would lead them. She wasn't going to get ahead of herself and wonder if there was going to be an introduction to each other's families, Dakota's parents, Simon…It was definitely much too early to think about that.

"Whatever happens, I have no regrets."

Dakota's face lit up at the blunt admission.

"Neither do I," she said.

It was a good start, Rae decided.

"Now take some of those pancakes. I know you want to."

"You are pretty good at figuring out what I want." Her tone, warm and dark, left no doubt that she wasn't talking about breakfast, but she took a piece anyway.

"Age. Experience. Can't beat that," Rae told her, satisfied with herself.

Now, if only they could make some more progress before leaving town.

It was hard to have secrets in a small town, Rae reflected when they met with the Sheriff of Oak Valley.

"You don't have to tell us twice," he said. "I'll have someone drive by Hannah's house." When Dakota raised her eyebrows, he added, "Of course, we're somewhat aware of her story. If that son of a bitch ever sets foot in town, he'll get what's coming to him. Excuse my language, ladies."

Rae couldn't care less about the language, the swearing or the patronizing.

"Those are strong words nonetheless. Has she mentioned her family?"

"Her brother who tried to poison her when they were kids? Yes, definitely. She became friends with one of my deputies, and she told us what she'd been through."

"Okay. I'm glad that she has someone to look out for her." The turn of events, however, created another problem. Under these circumstances, there was little chance they'd get to take a look at Hannah's phone records to get to her brother. They would have to find another way.

"I was hoping we could stay in contact. It's important that we talk to Martin Kinsley."

"Those basement murders? You think it's him?"

"We don't know yet," Rae reminded him, thinking he sounded a tad too enthusiastic.

She shared a look with Dakota who shrugged.

"I'll let you know if he turns up. What are we dealing with? Is he likely to be armed?"

She would have said no if it wasn't for the shooting at Trevor Gaines' place, and Cindy Lowman's violent kidnapping.

"I wouldn't rule anything out at his point. Mr. Kinsley is a person of interest, but whoever is behind the murders likely knows that we're getting closer. I want you and everyone involved to be careful and let us know the moment there's a sighting."

"Yes, Ma'am."

She hadn't missed Dakota's quick amused smile at his reaction. Suffice to say, the sheriff was not used to anyone telling him what to do, much less a woman who was apparently still used to being the boss.

"Thank you for your cooperation, Sheriff. We'll be in touch."

"Did you see his face?" Dakota asked when they were in the car, laughing. "Didn't call us ladies any longer."

"I don't really care what he calls me. I just want this to end. I think we're close."

"Yeah. If we find Martin Kinsley, we'll get more missing pieces of the story. The folks in Oak Valley seem very protective of Hannah. Either they have a reason, or she has fooled them. One way or another, we'll find out."

Rae smiled to herself, admitting that her hopeful attitude this morning didn't just stem from the progress they were making in the case, though it was a big part of it.

The fog was finally clearing.

Chapter 22

The text message Dakota received when they were back at work slightly dimmed her excellent mood. They had both gotten a change of clothes at their respective homes, and an angrily meowing Rex had been fed and provided with new water and litter.

Currently, Rae was updating Lieutenant Castillo in his office while Dakota was sorting out everything that had come to her desk in their absence.

The lab had found a match between the DNA sample found at Marla's house, and small blood specks taken from the apartment where Cindy had been held.

Did that mean the perpetrator was getting more careless? Feeling cornered? Her gaze went back to the message her mother had sent her.

Dinner tonight. Mona and Tim will join us, as we have some business to discuss. Will you be there?

On a whim, Dakota texted back, waiting for the answer. Perhaps she had stunned her mother into silence with her question?

She looked back at Castillo's office where he and Rae were apparently about to wrap up. A couple of minutes later, Rae left the office. Dakota's mother still hadn't answered. Perhaps she thought Dakota was joking.

"Okay, Baker is coming in later today, so when he's here, we can talk about..."

Her cell phone buzzed, interrupting Rae.

"...what he found on Kinsley. Unfortunately, I don't think it's an address, but we're getting closer."

Dakota's phone vibrated on her desk again.

"Do you need to get that?"

"Maybe I should. Sorry."

She picked up the phone and read the two recent messages.

That's a surprise.

Be there at six.

That was gracious. Dinners would usually start with a cocktail around four p.m., but even her family understood that her job wasn't nine to five, even less so at the moment.

"Bad news?" Rae asked, her concern warming Dakota. She shouldn't react that way, not after something that might lead nowhere. Something that happened in the perfect zone between comforting and blazing hot, for sure, but there was no guarantee, was there?"

"No," she said. "My parents are having dinner with Tim and Mona Bedford tonight. How would you feel about being my plus one?"

She could tell Rae was surprised. Dakota wasn't sure if it was a pleasant surprise, until she smiled.

"You're serious about that?"

"I so am. And there's something else I need to tell you later."

"You can tell me now." There was a question behind Rae's words, subtle enough not to be understood as criticism, but clearly a nudge. Dakota couldn't go there yet.

"Later. Please, trust me. I need to confirm something first."

It was beyond complicated, introducing Rae as her date to her parents, when she wasn't even certain they were dating, or if Rae was really thrilled to meet them, but she did like the idea.

Aside from that...She had found what had been nagging her ever since they'd met with Hannah Kinsley in person.

A huge airy office with lots of expensive art. It would be one hell of a coincidence, but there was definitely a connection to the university, and the means to pull off something like the incident at Gaines' and Cindy's abduction, all without getting his hands dirty.

The thought of what it all could mean terrified and infuriated her.

One way or another, they'd find out soon.

When she picked up Rae later that day, Dakota willed herself to give up on the nail-biting worry about how the evening might go. It could end up in an argument—par for the course for this kind of dinner. It could end up in a catastrophe, whether she was wrong or right.

But yes, she might be shallow too, because all her worries were out of the window the moment Rae greeted her at the door with a kiss. Getting a whiff of her perfume, Dakota resisted the impulse to sigh in bliss. She stepped back to admire her plus one, to the point where Rae asked, "Is this okay for a dinner? I wasn't sure, but based on what I saw at the Bedfords, and your apartment, I didn't want to take a chance."

"Don't worry. You look perfect."

She meant it, hadn't been this serious about anything in some time. Another scary subject. She was falling too hard, too fast. They were a long way from a crush already.

The blue dress Rae was wearing provided a beautiful contrast to her blonde hair and set off her eyes. It was a world away from Rae's more businesslike wear at work, luxurious. A part of her wanted to forget about dinner, especially given the complications it would bring without a doubt.

"That's high praise to live up to."

"Don't worry. You already do."

"Thank you. You look pretty perfect yourself." There was a hint of vulnerability to Rae's tone, a wistfulness. Dakota would have liked to ask her about it, but they'd be late, and that was practically the biggest sin you could commit in the Lord household. They had better not test fate.

"I'm glad you think so. The driver's waiting downstairs. Let's go."

Rae held her back, and Dakota wondered if she had the same thoughts about skipping dinner.

"Don't worry," Rae said. "It will be fine."

Dakota hoped she was right. Rae's hand on her back dissolved some of the tension that had settled in her body since she had made the connection.

Dakota hadn't missed Mona's mumbled "You've got to be kidding me." Regardless, she, Tim, and Dakota's parents stayed polite when she introduced Rae. The curiosity in the room was palpable, but as Dakota had expected, Rae stayed unfazed, acting like a mid-week dinner with obscenely wealthy people was a normal thing.

She was that good. Dakota suppressed a smile, reminding herself that they weren't here in a private capacity only. Any reflections on other things Rae excelled at were inappropriate.

"Thank you so much for having me," Rae said, her charming demeanor clearly distracting Dakota's parents from the many questions they wanted to ask.

"Oh, it's our pleasure," her mother said. "As you can see, we are having old friends of Dakota's over, and we don't see her often enough as it is. I'm glad you're here. How about a cocktail? My staff can mix you anything. Or wine?"

Dakota caught Rae's questioning gaze, and she nodded.

"Wine for me, please."

"I'll have the same," Rae said. "Thank you."

Tonight wasn't going to end in an arrest, just likely uncomfortable conversations.

How was she going to do this?

She knew she wasn't wrong, but the possible conclusions to draw were impossible, unreal. She could only hope that the murderer had the means to frame a lot of people—even rich ones. Otherwise...

When they were sitting in the spacious den, each of them provided with a glass of wine, Dakota caught a quick glance at Tim. She barely knew him, but she had been in his office a couple of times.

It was impressive, even to someone like Dakota who was no stranger to these kinds of spaces. Giant floor to ceiling windows that provided stellar views, artwork that cost more than what some of her colleagues made in a year. She had always assumed that Tim, like Mona, like herself, had been born into that kind of wealth. Was that really the case?

She remembered the single shard of green glass on display in a vitrine.

"Yes, it has meaning," he'd once told her, but never elaborated on it. Once Dakota remembered, she had realized that Hannah's eyes reminded her of someone: Tim Bedford. She might be tired, distracted, but she couldn't deny those pieces coming together.

And at the very least, Tim had to answer some questions.

There was no chance before or during dinner. At least, her parents seemed to be in a conciliatory mood. They didn't raise the question whether she was ever going to leave "that job" and come back to the business.

Dakota was grateful for Rae's ability to adjust quickly to this complex environment. She was so tired, but they were entering a crucial phase of the case.

The killer might be someone she had known for years.

When someone from the butler's staff came by, she accepted another glass of wine. She couldn't drink too much—she had to see this through.

"I like her," her mother said next to her. "But isn't she a bit old for you?"

It wouldn't be dinner if there was no comment on her professional or private life.

"Mom," she said wearily.

"Yes, I know, you're an adult. Just saying. If you still wanted children, you have to take that into consideration. I was one of the oldest moms when you went to elementary school, and that wasn't always fun."

"Sorry about that." She nearly laughed, first of all because her parents' timing certainly wasn't her fault, second, because she didn't think she or Rae would talk about children anytime soon—or ever.

Rae already had a child she needed to consider, and maybe, sometime in the future, he'd be a consideration for Dakota too. For a few heartbeats, she allowed herself the fantasy of the two of them walking down the Champs-Elysées, having a picnic near the Eiffel Tower, or sitting on a balcony of an apartment with a view.

"Well, what's done is done. Does she have children?"

"A son," Dakota replied, and, seeing that Tim had gotten up to go smoke outside, she added, "Excuse me?"

She waited another second or so before she followed him onto the balcony from which they had a view of the city in the distance.

"I didn't know you smoked," he said, holding out a pack of cigarettes to her.

"No, thank you. I don't."

She let the silence drag on for almost a minute, testing his reaction.

He gave her an amused smile.

"So, you brought your new girlfriend to dinner. That's brave. You saw Mona shooting daggers at her, and your parents were surprised to say the least."

Dakota shrugged. "Everyone will get over it. I didn't mean to provoke. Mom's right, I don't often have time, and it's nice to see everyone. Mona and I are still friends."

Somewhat. Acquaintances was more like it, since Mona considered her profession and circle too working class for her tastes, but he didn't need to know that.

"Good for you," he said. "I don't think that I could do your job. It's got to be tough."

"Sometimes," she admitted. "I was thinking about something you said a while ago. I was looking for some decoration for my apartment, and that reminded me of the sculpture you have in your office. The green shard."

"Oh, that."

Apparently, he was still not eager to divulge any deeper meaning attached to it.

"Yeah. I always liked it. Simple, clean...You never said where it came from."

"I didn't." The humor was gone from his tone. "There's no big revelation here. It's a reminder of what is possible. You can go from a piece of broken glass to something pretty decent."

"I like that metaphor."

He laughed at that. "I'm afraid it's not a metaphor. I think it came from a broken glass bottle. I got it cleaned up and put in my office the day I moved in."

Dakota took a deep breath before she said, "Hannah told me about the shard. I'm really sorry about what happened. That must have been hard, but you made it out."

"And there I thought they gave you a badge because you're pretty."

"Not funny, but given the subject matter, I think I'll have to forgive you. Tim, we need to talk."

"About that shard? I think you'd be better off hiring a designer than asking me for décor inspiration."

"About the shard and other things. I came out here, so we don't have to do this in front of Mona and my parents. I'd like you to come in tomorrow."

"Come in where...Really, Dakota? This is ridiculous. My father almost killed my mother. My sister and I went into foster care, and I won the lottery. There's nothing illegal about that."

"We talked to Hannah," she said, "and we need to clear up a few things. It should be fast."

He shook his head. "Whatever it is you think I did, you're wrong. I have some stories to tell you about Hannah. Fine, I'll come in tomorrow."

"Thank you. I want this over as much as you do."

Tim held her gaze long enough for the moment to turn uncomfortable.

"I guess you do. I'll see you tomorrow, then. I hope you're ready for the truth."

Dakota had never been more ready for this case to end, but she had succeeded.

Chapter 23

Dakota's demeanor didn't reveal anything about how the conversation had gone as long as they were still at her parents' home. Tim Bedford kept a poker face as well, and so it wasn't until they were in the car that Rae learned the details.

She had mixed feelings about Dakota's approach, a lot of them inappropriate protectiveness.

"That was a risk, to confront him this directly." She didn't mean to chide her. Dakota knew how to do her job, and she'd done it for some time before Rae came along. Still. If they were right, this man had murdered two women and was responsible for the attack in Gaines' apartment and Lowman's kidnapping. She wasn't going to take any chances.

"I didn't spook him if that's what you mean. He has too high a profile to disappear. Besides I think he enjoyed it quite a bit."

It was not encouraging to hear that a potential murderer enjoyed a cat-and-mouse game, but Rae didn't want Dakota to misinterpret her words.

"I didn't say that. He might be the shooter or the one who paid him. That's all I'm saying."

She didn't miss Dakota flinch.

"We're going to clear this up tomorrow, I swear. I wonder if someone was trying to set him up. He's got to have a lot of enemies."

"That would be quite an elaborate scheme," Rae mused.

"Yeah. I won't argue with you on that."

She sounded tired, and at a red light, Rae took her hand, squeezing it gently.

"We'll figure it out."

Dakota gave her a grateful smile.

"How long have you known the family?"

"Ten, twelve years maybe, since they and my parents started doing business. I don't know Tim that well, but no one ever talked about him being adopted. He didn't deny that the green shard came from that basement, on the contrary. Are we still looking in the wrong place?"

"What if we aren't?" Rae asked softly. "That's going to be tough on your family...on you?"

"Like I said, I don't know him well. It would certainly be a shock for everyone, but that can't keep us from doing our jobs, can it?"

"You're right."

"You want to come up?" Dakota asked when they arrived at her building, drawing Rae into a world of temptation. She really wanted to. Practical and responsible Rae won, just barely.

"I can't. I'm supposed to talk to Gen and Simon early tomorrow morning."

Studying Dakota closely, she found a hint of disappointment in her expression.

"Another time then."

"Yes, definitely."

"Tomorrow bright and early." When Dakota leaned in to kiss her, Rae questioned her decision. But keeping up those conversations mattered. If Dakota was going to be in her life, they'd both have to work with these realities.

Just like Rae had to accept the reality that the new woman in her life came from more riches than she imagined.

Tim Bedford. Rae sat with her laptop until late that night, doing some additional research. What had led them to him was all a series of coincidences. If he was indeed Martin Kinsley, his adoptive parents had made sure to wipe the slate clean for him.

Because of the accusations looming over him?

He had changed his looks quite drastically since the last picture they had of Kinsley. It was no wonder that it had taken Dakota this long to make the connection.

But what if it was all a tragic misunderstanding? Would they still assume that Kinsley/Bedford was the one? In any case, the setting fit. Creepy basements. Abusive families. Hannah's dolls.

They would make sense of it one way or another.

She absent-mindedly petted Rex who had jumped into her lap. After a short period of resentment, he had come to show his appreciation for her presence.

"Yes, I know it's late," she said when he meowed softly. "We should call it a night, and continue this tomorrow, right? He will have some answers for us."

Rex looked at her as if he doubted her words, though Rae couldn't be sure which part. She suppressed a yawn and closed her laptop.

The alarm would ring too soon.

Later, she lay awake nonetheless, chiding herself thinking she could have spent the time differently. The fantasy of taking the satiny violet dress off Dakota was the second-best thing, keeping her company until she fell asleep.

In the morning, she hurried to get ready so she could have breakfast and catch Genevieve and Simon at lunch.

"What the..." She stopped herself short of swearing when she saw the bruise on Simon's face. "What happened to you? Are you okay?"

"I'm fine, Mom," he chirped, his French accent a bit more pronounced than she remembered. "Just a little bike accident."

"Well, enough to almost give me a heart attack," Genevieve mumbled, "but he's right. He's fine now, no broken bones. We're fine. What about you?"

"I..." Rae wasn't sure what to say. Her heart was slowly starting to beat normal again, but she couldn't help feeling sad for all the moments she had already missed, and the ones to come. Had Gen assured him that it was okay to cry? "I'm okay." She hadn't mentioned the shooting, or her subsequent road trip with Dakota. Rae wasn't sure she wanted to, especially in front of Simon.

"I'm really sorry this happened, but you've got to be careful, okay?"

"Sure. My soccer team won the finals!"

"You did! Wow, that's amazing!" Her coffee was getting cold, but Rae didn't mind. She could—and would—always get more later. "I wish I could have been there."

"Me too."

She searched for any hint of a jibe but couldn't find any. Simon wasn't one to hold back.

"I wish you could come visit us."

"I'm working on it, sweetheart." Now he wrinkled his nose a bit at the endearment. "I swear I'll figure something out. Maybe during your summer vacation."

It hurt her heart how his face lit up at the idea. She couldn't just make promises. She *had* to figure something out. Rae cast a regretful look at the small clock in the corner of the screen.

"I'm afraid I have to go now. Enjoy your lunch. I'll talk to my boss when he has a moment."

She wasn't sure how he'd react to her taking a vacation when she'd just joined, but with a little luck, she and Dakota would soon close a high-profile case.

Maybe, just maybe...but she was getting too far ahead of herself.

"I'll see you soon. Love you."

"Love you too, Mom," Simon echoed while Gen looked pensive.

Rae had another mystery to solve first.

Tim Bedford arrived at the station twelve minutes late. He didn't apologize. Rae wasn't going to take the bait, but she knew, a lot depended on the outcome of this conversation. That's what they were calling it for now.

Mark had warned them that they needed something tangible.

Rae was determined to provide it if there was something to find.

Dakota appeared calm, but her hands were cold when Rae took them in an earlier, stolen moment before they got ready. She felt warmed and thrilled remembering the gentle intimacy, but she had to push it far from her mind now.

"Mr. Bedford, thank you for making time for us. There are just a few questions we need to clear up. Come with us, please?"

"Not a problem. Dakota's parents have been long-time friends of mine, and perhaps you know that there's history between her and my sister."

Rae had no doubt that every word and gesture was intentional. Dakota's lips thinned, but she didn't say anything.

They settled in an interrogation room. Bedford's jovial smile didn't falter.

"This is all very interesting. Like on TV. But I'm curious how my crappy family history can help you in any way."

He and Dakota sat on opposite sides of the table. Rae remained standing.

"It will be clearer soon, I promise. I just want to let you know we are recording this conversation, in case you should need it later."

"It *is* like on TV." He laughed. "So, Dakota told me you talked to Hannah. I can only imagine the stories she told you."

"You've been in touch lately?"

"I don't care to be. She's from another life, one that I don't care looking back on."

"Yet, you kept a reminder."

"Yes, to remind myself to be grateful for each day I come to my office. I changed my name legally. That time...it doesn't even exist anymore."

"No one should have to live like you and your sister did, and I'm sorry. I can only imagine you felt responsible for Hannah, to make sure she ate when your mother couldn't or wouldn't take care of these things."

She saw his eyes narrow. Rae had expected that kind of reaction at the mention of Mrs. Kinsley.

"Who cares anymore? She's God knows where, my biological father is dead, and Hannah..." He snickered. "Well, you met Hannah."

"Do you remember the dolls?" Dakota's soft-spoken question cut through the polite air as Bedford realized they weren't just here for an amiable chat.

"What does that have to do with anything? They were creepy too, but Hannah loved them. I guess that tells you something."

"You reacted quite differently to your ordeal. It must have been hard, trying to protect your sister when you had no help from any adult."

Bedford made a show of looking at his watch.

"Yeah, had therapy, blah blah. No need to regurgitate it. Is there anything else you'd like to ask me? Otherwise, I'm leaving."

"I'd like you to look at these two dates and tell us where you were. I imagine it will be quick and easy to clear that up."

Impatient, he glanced at the sheet Dakota laid in front of him.

"I was either at the office or at home."

"Is there security footage at the office that could tell us when you left?"

He stared back at Dakota, starting to laugh.

"Look, I indulged this long enough because I know your parents, and because of that ill-fated fling with Mona she keeps talking about when she's drunk. She remembers you fondly," he said with a grin that made Rae take a step forward.

"If there's any problem with your alibi, we'll likely have more questions, Mr. Bedford. I'm sorry, but that's how it works. So, can you provide us with any security footage?"

He got to his feet.

"This is outrageous. I'm not going to provide you with anything unless you present a warrant to my lawyers. Thank you, ladies. It's been fun."

"Let me see you out," Dakota offered, and he didn't object. Rae stayed behind, contemplating what they'd just heard, and wondering if it had moved the needle at all. Tim Bedford was Martin Kinsley. Was he also a killer? She cast a glance at the half-empty coffee cup he'd left behind. They might know more soon.

Dakota returned to the room a few minutes later.

"That went well," she said with a sigh.

"Do you still think he's innocent?" Rae knew Dakota still had doubts, reasonable ones as well. Just because everything fit together so well in theory, it didn't mean it was the truth. But they had the means to further rule him out.

"I don't know, but let's get that coffee cup to the lab just in case."

"You know what's going to happen if it's a match, right?"

Dakota gave her a wry smile. "I've been around people like that, and their lawyers, all my life. Of course they'll try to throw it out, and they'd be right since he didn't give his consent...We just have to find more."

"Easier said than done. Okay, let's get this done."

Chapter 24

They had to wait once more. Dakota admitted to herself that this was the part of the job she disliked the most. Whenever things moved, they came closer to providing justice for the victims—moments like these, stalled, all she could do was think of missed opportunities and failures.

Until now, anyway.

Tomorrow, Rae didn't have an early morning call with her ex and son.

Tonight, she was doing her best to distract Dakota from her frustrations about work and anything going on outside this bedroom.

This was the opposite of frustration. Her mind clear and open, she had no trouble surrendering to perfect bliss.

It didn't last.

"Castillo wasn't too happy with the results, was he?"

"He agrees that we have to wait." To her credit, Rae didn't sound annoyed, just pensive, her hand still playing with Dakota's hair.

"I hate this. I mean...He's not my friend, but someone I've known for years. That is not great. The other side is that we are giving him too much leeway. He covered up his entire past. How do we know he won't jump on a private jet and disappear?"

"His alibi checked out," Rae reminded her. In lieu of footage, they had checked in with staff who had confirmed Bedford had stayed at the office past the time of death determined for both Sarah and Marla. What did it really mean? He could have given them the poison and left. Snuck away without being seen?

"So, it's either that, or we'll have to start over?"

"I don't think so. All we have to do is wait a bit longer. When the DNA results come in, we bring him in again. That will rattle him."

How could she be so confident?

"I can't wait for this to be over," Dakota admitted. "I'm thinking a vacation is in order."

"Yeah, that would be nice."

For a moment, the silence was full of opportunity, but Rae didn't elaborate, about a vacation together, perhaps in Paris. Dakota reasoned that it was much too early to imagine meeting her son—or Genevieve. She seemed to have her life together a whole lot more than Mona. That shouldn't be intimidating, though it was, to some extent. Rae had shared so much more with her than Dakota had with Mona. Exes or not, she couldn't ignore that, whatever was in the future for them.

Better not to mention it.

She had a surprisingly good night's sleep at Rae's despite everything on her mind. In the morning, they had no news from the lab yet, so they indulged in breakfast at home. Dakota had brought a change of clothes with her this time. Sitting in Rae's sun-filled kitchen, Rex curled up on the chair next to her, she felt more at ease than she had in a while.

"My parents really liked you," she said, wondering where that wistful tone came from, or if she was crazy to mention this now. Would Rae care? They still hadn't determined what this, between them, was.

"They were nice," Rae conceded. "I guess things might not be so pleasant once they talk to the Bedfords. I'm sorry."

"Well...I expected that. It's more important that we get to the truth."

"That it is," Rae said calmly.

She should have left it at that, enjoy coffee and the pastry that was not part of her usual breakfast, but Dakota couldn't help it.

"So, when am I going to meet your parents?" Teasing. Perhaps she was a bit serious.

"Well, you can't meet my dad, except at the cemetery."

"Oh my God, I'm so sorry."

"Don't be. It's been a few years. You couldn't know."

Yet there was a hint of pain to Rae's voice.

"My mom is alive and well though. She lives a couple of hours away." Rae shook her head with a smile. "We don't have to have this conversation, not now. It's fine to take it slow and see where this leads us..."

It may not have been the exact answer Dakota had wanted to hear, but she could live with it. She had no choice either since Rae's phone rang.

"The lab," she mouthed, before she said, "Yes, I'm listening. Okay, we'll be right there. Thank you."

Rae ended the call. Dakota couldn't quite decipher her expression, but her words left no doubt. "We have a match." She paused for a beat. "While this is exciting, I also know it's not easy for you. I'm sorry."

"Thank you, but don't be." Dakota got to her feet. "It's going to be unpleasant, yes. It's more important that we finally catch him."

"Agreed. Now let's get ourselves some warrants."

The DNA match was indeed enough to grant them a warrant for Bedford's commercial space and private residence.

They caught him at home over breakfast. Tim Bedford seemed strangely unaffected.

"You know, Dakota, I never thought you were petty. If you wanted to get back at Mona for dumping you, there would have been other ways."

Dakota caught Rae's questioning look and shrugged.

"Whatever you say."

He shook his head, his tone patronizing as he said, "You know your parents are going to hear about this."

"Oh, I know."

"That doesn't bother you?"

"They don't have a say in how I do my job. The judge who signed off on this warrant, does. Now can we do this?"

He gave an exaggerated shrug. "Help yourself, ladies. I have nothing to hide, though I have to mention your little stunt will cost me a lot of money."

Rae gave him a polite smile. Dakota was sure she wanted to roll her eyes instead.

"We are very sorry for the inconvenience, Mr. Bedford. While we're here, could you confirm something for us? I seem to remember you said you never went to Sarah Cooper's home."

"That's right. Why would I go there? We met at her office at the university, or mine at the company. We didn't see each other socially."

"Your relationship was strictly professional, then."

"I believe that's what I said. Crime must be really slow if you are this bored."

Rae chose to ignore the accusation.

"Well, thank you. We'll have to ask you to go outside. We will get back to you as soon as anything changes."

"This is unbelievable." He followed their orders though. "I am calling my lawyer."

"You are entitled to do that," Rae told him. "What a charming young man," she added when he had left the room. "I understand why you kept your distance."

Dakota appreciated her not mentioning that she had failed to keep her distance from another Bedford. That gave her an idea.

"Yeah. Maybe I was just lucky. Could you handle this for the moment? I'd like to check something."

Either Tim had simply tried to get a rise out of her by saying Mona was the one who had ended their relationship, or Mona was telling various untrue versions about their break-up. Maybe she could use it to her advantage. It was worth a try.

Mona was in her office, amused when she saw Dakota.

"Of course you walked straight past my secretary. Like the old days."

"Good morning, Mona. This is serious. We got a search warrant for your brother's house." And more than that, but those were semantics at the moment.

"So I've heard. I have to say, you have a lot of nerve coming here. My parents are livid, and they have been on the phone with your parents."

Dakota had to laugh, even though she had expected the constant mention of her family when she told Rae the morning was going to be unpleasant.

"Yeah, I figured that. And speaking of a game of telephone, what was it again, you dumped me, or you can't get over me? Tim's words, not mine."

Mona rolled her eyes, though Dakota wasn't sure if it was for her or her brother.

"I'm sorry," she said. "But I need your help. It's important."

"You're turning our lives upside down. Don't you have what you need already?"

"We know that Tim changed his name with the help of your parents. His name was Martin Kinsley before your parents adopted him."

"Yeah, so? I thought you knew. About the adoption anyway."

"I didn't, but that's beside the point. What I wanted to hear from you was your impression, anything you remember. Did Tim have any problems as a teenager? Anything relating to violence?"

Mona's eyes widened.

"What are you saying? That's outrageous. He never touched me—or anyone else. He was pretty shy, always had his nose in a book."

Dakota hadn't missed the way she had worded her statement. Was that emotion concern for her family, or was she afraid Dakota might find out a secret?

"Okay. Are you sure? You can tell me."

"There's nothing to tell."

"His sister accused him of wanting to poison her. He was ten, eleven at the time."

"And she was even younger, right? I don't know the whole story, but from what I've picked up here and there I could tell they lived under pretty shitty circumstances. You don't think it's possible she made that up? She got sick and invented a story around it?"

"We are looking into all the possibilities right now."

"Are you? You seem to have made up your mind that my brother is a murdering predator."

Dakota had to admit that here in this place where she'd spent a lot of time, with the woman she'd once dated, Tim's sister, it didn't seem to make a lot of sense. But DNA didn't lie, and Tim's/Martin's DNA had been found in a dead woman's apartment, a place he swore he'd never been.

Something didn't add up.

"That's not what I said. Mona, this is serious."

"If you have enough on him, what do you need me for?"

"Did he ever talk about his other family? His sister Hannah?" Dakota pressed.

"To Mom and Dad, and the therapist they got him, yes, I assume, because he had no choice. To me, no, he never spoke of them at all."

It was not surprising, and yet disconcerting.

"He said he wanted a clean slate," Dakota remembered.

"Can you blame him?"

"Do you have any idea why your parents didn't adopt Hannah as well?"

"She was with another family, and doing okay," Mona answered. "I don't think they were ever that close, so it worked out for both of them."

Did it? It made the theory that he had wanted to protect his young sister less likely.

"Are we done? As much as I enjoy chatting with you, I need to go back to work."

How did they always make it about their time, and their money?

Dakota had to call Detective Baker.

When she arrived at the station, Rae was still at Tim Bedford's house. She found Baker at his desk, and he produced the information she was looking for. They had addresses for the group homes the siblings had stayed at, but the one where Tim had lived after being rescued from his parents' home didn't exist anymore, and the staff of the house where Hannah had been all those years ago was too young to remember her.

Still, she thought this was an important avenue.

"We'll have to continue with Bedford. Stay on this, please, and let me know if you can track down any of them. Hannah said she didn't want to be in the same home as Martin. Someone has to remember."

"Sure." He didn't voice the doubts obvious in his expression.

Dakota went to her own desk from where she called Rae.

Chapter 25

Bedford knew they were looking for a needle in a haystack. Rae was determined to look hard, and not just because she didn't like him.

She *didn't* like him. He was acting like the archetypal rich and arrogant guy, his attempts at getting Dakota flustered obvious and bordering on embarrassing.

She didn't get flustered easily.

Rae directed her focus back to the information in front of her. They could trace Bedford's days fairly easily. His alibi still held, which was troubling her. He could pay a lot of people if he wanted to, and the person who had committed the murders had to be someone with extensive resources.

"How's it going?"

She looked up to see Mark standing in front of her desk.

"It's going," she said.

"Anything concrete yet?"

"That would be a no."

Rae didn't blame him for the stressed tone in his voice. A lot depended on the outcome of this search. As a lieutenant, she had seen confrontations with rich suspects who thought they should be above the law. Bedford was wealthier than anyone she'd dealt with. "If this doesn't lead to an arrest, we'll have a problem." She didn't even try phrasing it as a question. Not only would she and Dakota have to go back to square one—which would be frustrating enough even if she wasn't dreaming about Paris—but Mark would likely take a lot of heat too. Bedford senior probably played golf with the mayor.

"That's a polite way of phrasing it," he said with a sigh. "What is your gut telling you?"

"We're going to need a bit more than my gut feeling—"

"Rae."

"I think he did it, and I think Dakota would say the same. We just have to prove it. I mean we could bring him in again based on the DNA results, but for how long..."

"Find me something," he urged. "Where is Lord, by the way?"

"Following a lead." She had spoken to Baker earlier, but Rae hadn't seen her since they'd parted at Bedford's home.

"This is more important than anything. She should be here."

Reading the room, Rae picked up her phone. "I'll call her."

"You do that. And let me know the moment you find something."

"Will do, sir," she said, but his tense expression remained.

"Thanks." He turned around and went back to his office.

Rae's call went to voicemail. She left a message and went back to work.

Dakota had returned by the time a lab technician informed them on the findings from Bedford's phone records.

More pieces were coming together: Even though staff had confirmed his alibi for the nights Sarah and Marla had died, his private phone showed up in the vicinity of both residences.

Dakota groaned. "The lawyer's just going to argue someone took his phone and is trying to frame him. Same with the DNA."

Rae understood her frustration. Since she'd returned, they had been at this for hours, phone records, bank statements, every scrap of paper and file that related to donations to the university and business with Sarah. They couldn't prove that he had met Marla.

"Hey, I see you're still at it," Baker commented.

Dakota all but jumped to her feet. Rae hid a smile at her eagerness. She could keep her adoration mostly to herself, but moments like this...

"You have something for us?"

"I think so," he said. "Opinions on Mr. Kinsley were pretty clear. Since we're all here a bit longer, what about food? Pizza?"

"I'll pay if you order," Dakota declared. "Rae and I will set up in the breakroom. We'll see you over there."

"Um, wait, what do you want?"

"Hawaiian," Dakota said, and to Rae, "Are you coming?"

"Margherita, please." She followed Dakota into the breakroom. When they had closed the door behind them, she stated, "You must be really hungry. Also, pineapple..."

"No jokes about that," Dakota returned, and the next moment her mouth was on Rae's. She indulged both of them for long enough to be careless, because anyone could walk in on them...For a few heartbeats, she didn't care.

"Okay." She stepped back, still breathless. "We might have to talk about the separation of private and professional...and your pizza choices."

"You're not serious." Dakota's smile was downright smug.

"No, not really. About the pizza anyway. But it's been a long day, and I understand..."

"Being hungry?"

"Don't tempt me."

Dakota was still wearing that smile when Baker walked in.

"What did I miss?"

"Nothing," they said in perfect unison.

"I don't think I want to know. You, however, settle in. I was able to find a couple of former staff, and they definitely had stories to tell. It seems like Martin Kinsley is not the type of kid you ever forget."

Dakota's expression had changed. "I talked to Mona Bedford earlier. She claims she can't remember him getting into trouble as a teen, but I found it hard to believe her. I don't know. I never had the feeling before that she was scared of him, but today, I got that impression."

"You want to hear the story or not?"

Dakota motioned for him to go ahead.

"All right. So, for some reason, the siblings were separated once they got out of that house. Sister was in the hospital for a few days, mostly for malnutrition. We don't know if Martin tried to poison her, but she was discharged pretty quick, and then the Bedfords came along."

"Wait, what? Didn't Hannah say she was adopted before him?" Dakota asked, frowning.

"Technically, she was. The Bedfords would have taken them both in, but she refused to go anywhere Martin went. That's what the staff member told us. By the time they had all the paperwork together, including Martin's name change, Hannah was already living with another family."

"This is strange. Who signed off on all of this? And why?"

"Someone who believed her but had no proof?" Dakota suggested.

"There's more," Baker continued. "During the time Kinsley was at the home, two girls disappeared."

"Fuck," Dakota mumbled. Rae didn't have a more accurate statement to describe the situation. If they were right, not only had he killed before, but he had done so numerous times, his resources constantly increasing by the time he was able to leave his biological family behind. The number of victims…

"I want to check in with Hannah," she said. "Just to be on the safe side."

Even though Hannah didn't report anything out of the ordinary, sleep didn't come easily that night. The coming day would have been enough to keep them up. The other reason was entirely their fault, Rae thought, smiling in the dark, long after Dakota had fallen asleep in her arms. She was confident that between the DNA results, more of Tim Bedford's history, and his ego, they'd get closer to the truth.

She allowed herself to dream of something that was not yet palpable, Paris, introducing Dakota to Simon, and well, of course Gen. She couldn't help frowning thinking of Dakota's parents. She hoped it would go better with her own family.

Rae had easily seen past the Lords' polite façade, which was clearly not just about her age. That was something they would probably frown upon in private. No matter how much of an effort she'd made to dress appropriately for the occasion, they could likely sense that socializing with people like them was not the norm for her.

She could still see something of a future with Dakota. She wanted it. She was already scared of losing it.

Chapter 26

Dakota woke from the sound of soft voices, wildly opposing impulses warring in her mind. She was curious. She wanted to stay in the warmth of the soft sheets, for Rae to come back to her, preferably never leave this space.

She had tried her best to play it cool, but Rae's gentle nudges showed her that she saw through her. No, it wasn't easy. Yes, her parents would be shocked, after they got past their silent rage that Dakota dared to go after one of their own. Because for years, the Bedford's children's lives had fit their mold so much better than Dakota's. Well, Tim, anyway, because he was straight, and the pursuit of more wealth was everything that mattered to him.

Tim. Martin, who had allegedly poisoned his sister, in whose vicinity two girls had disappeared.

She was awake now. Dakota picked up her satin robe—these days, she packed a proper overnight bag when staying at Rae's. When did that happen?

She went over to the kitchen, tempted by the scent of coffee, and Rae, still comfortably dressed in a tank top and PJ bottoms as she sat in front of her laptop, chatting with her family across the pond.

Dakota was secretly thrilled when Rae interrupted her conversation to smile at her over the edge of her screen before she went back to the subject matter at hand.

"No, I haven't asked my boss yet," she said. "We're in a critical phase with the case. I'll know more soon. I promise."

"You said that the last time, Mom." The boy sounded disappointed. Dakota could sympathize. She wondered if Rae would introduce her, but then she remembered she wasn't wearing anything but panties and a satin robe...probably not appropriate for such an occasion.

"I have to go," Rae said. "I'll call again soon, I promise."

Dakota could have interpreted her words in various ways. She might want to talk about the case some more, have a relaxed breakfast with her, as relaxed as it could be under the circumstances. As it was, Dakota wondered if she was cutting the conversation short because she wasn't ready to tell them that she'd had a guest. Overnight. Again.

Silly to be worried about that, wasn't it? They were adults. Rae wasn't obliged to cater to her insecurities. Especially when they were unfounded. Reflecting on last night, Dakota decided they were, in fact, unfounded.

"What's the smile for?" Rae asked.

"Us being efficient," she returned. "We're going to solve this today."

Rae's expression turned doubtful in the face of this much optimism.

"One can only hope. It's unbelievable that he has managed to get away with this for so long."

"Not much longer," Dakota said, determined. "I'm tired of dreaming of creepy dolls too."

Rae got up from where she was sitting at the table and wordlessly pulled her close.

The nightmare would end.

"You didn't want me to say hello?"

She couldn't help it. Her mother had said a long time ago that she could never leave well enough alone. In her family, it hadn't been a welcome trait. It made her a good investigator. It wasn't always helpful in relationships.

Rae's expression was unreadable, a bit surprised perhaps.

"Did you want to?"

"I don't know. I don't like secrets. And I want to avoid things getting awkward in the future."

"They're not awkward. Gen is seeing someone. Does that mean you want us to go to HR?"

Was she serious? The problem was, Dakota didn't know what she wanted. Everything about Rae, with Rae, had happened fast, and the intensity of the feelings she had for her, a woman divorced with a child, troubled her. She figured there was about fourteen, fifteen years between them, years of experience, on the job, in life.

She felt safe with Rae. She felt challenged like never before.

"I didn't say that. But..." *I'd like to go to Paris with you, and your family should know who I am to you before that?*

"But what?"

"Nothing. We need to focus. If we play our cards right, he might realize that there's no way out of this."

"Dakota." Rae's tone was patient. "If there's something we should talk about right now, a few minutes certainly won't make a difference."

"They might. Let's do this first."

At Bedford's home, the housekeeper informed them that he had left early for the office. Dakota had a bad feeling. She could tell from Rae's pensive expression that she was considering all the options too. Best case scenario, he was hiding out with his lawyers, discussing a pre-emptive strategy. Something told her that might not be the case.

They had taken their respective cars, and when Dakota arrived at Bedford's company, Rae was already standing in the lobby. Frustrated had replaced pensive.

Dakota's heart sank. Had they waited too long?

"He's not here," Rae said. "Could you call Mona and his parents? I'll check with Hannah again, and if that doesn't do it, we'll get a BOLO out."

Dakota felt a chill skitter down her spine.

"It's time for that?"

"Yes, I believe so. We still only have bits and pieces, but there are too many of them."

"I agree."

The Bedfords didn't pick up, so Dakota left a message. Mona's greeting was a groan.

"You again. What do you want?"

"I need to speak to Tim. It's urgent."

"Why are you calling me then?"

"He's not at home or at his office. He's not picking up his phone either."

"Then I assume he's busy and doesn't want to talk to you?"

"Mona, this isn't a joke. We need to find him!"

"Yeah, well, he's not here and I haven't heard from him. If I do, I'll let you know. Have a good day, Dakota."

Dakota doubted that she was serious about any of it, but she had bigger problems. When she looked at Rae, she was startled by the worry in her eyes.

"I can't reach Hannah either. I'm calling the sheriff."

"One of us should go, then?"

"You're right. I'll go. Okay, I want you to go back and bring Mark and Baker up to speed."

Dakota noticed vaguely that she still called her old partner by his first name, even though he was both their boss now. Rae didn't make connections on a whim, and she valued the ones she had. Ex-partners.

"Will do."

"I'll check in with you."

"You think that's where he's going? Some sort of final act?"

"I think he's smarter than that," Rae conceded. "But just in case, I want everyone prepared."

"Okay then."

Dakota didn't think they'd pick up the conversation from this morning anytime soon. Maybe it was better that way. She was okay with casual meanwhile. Wasn't she?

Dakota all but jogged back to her car. While she understood Rae's reasoning, she felt uneasy about letting her go back to see Hannah alone. She sat in the driver's seat, put on the seatbelt, and took a deep breath. Rae knew what she was doing. She would certainly check in with the sheriff first, not go off on her own...The way Dakota had on a few occasions.

No, Rae was sensible above all. She didn't need to worry about her.

Now, both their jobs were to find Tim and explain to the lieutenant why he had been able to slip away.

Dakota jumped when she thought she'd seen movement in the rearview mirror. Get a grip. That was impossible. Things like that only happened in the movies...

The next moment she felt the sting of a needle in her neck, flailing as the fast-acting drug took effect, making her breathless and dizzy within seconds. The figure behind her, wearing a dark jacket and a baseball cap, blurred in the mirror.

Fuck.

She remembered Bedford senior once saying that he didn't like it when women, especially young attractive women, cursed.

Would he find the fact that his adoptive son was a murderer, less offensive?

It was her last thought before consciousness slipped away.

Chapter 27

Hannah and the sheriff had assured her that things were calm. Still, Rae didn't regret talking to both in person.

She preferred to be on the safe side, and she didn't care that both seemed to think she was paranoid, thinking that Tim Bedford's next target could be his biological sister, his originally intended victim.

"Let him come here," Hannah said darkly. "I have a gun."

"I spoke to the sheriff. You'll be protected."

"Well. Thanks. You didn't need to come all the way here to tell me that."

After returning to her car, Rae checked her phone, surprised to find no messages from either Dakota or Mark. She hoped that might mean good news, and that they had found Bedford already. Things could happen very fast from there. She was ready for the rush of a case coming to a close, justice served...

And perhaps she and Dakota could celebrate together. If the latter was still interested. She frowned at remembering their earlier conversation. What did those little hints between the lines mean? She couldn't quite figure out what Dakota seemed to be so worried about. Once they turned off the lights, there were no doubts or misunderstandings in their communication.

Rae appreciated that reality, more than anything. She'd had the dream of the perfect wedding a happily ever after, a typical family…Not everything had turned out that way. She and Dakota might have had a rocky start to their professional relationship, but she appreciated the more casual but passionate connection.

At this point in her life, it suited her perfectly, and someone as young as Dakota wouldn't be concerned about things not going fast enough, would she?

Well, there was one way to find out. Maybe tonight.

She picked up and called her, surprised when the call went to voicemail. Dakota expected her call, didn't she? Rae had only sent one text message on the way, and one after assuring herself that the sheriff's department was ready for all eventualities.

She tried Mark Castillo's number. He picked up after three rings.

"Rae, where are you?"

"I'm on my way back. I should be there in half an hour."

"Back from where?" He sounded frustrated.

"Mark, what's going on? Didn't Dakota tell you? Bedford is on the run. I had to see Hannah and the sheriff to make sure everything was in place. They are prepared."

"Rae."

"Yes, I know, but where else would he go? He knows he's cornered."

"Will you listen to me for a second?"

That silenced her. Rae had the uncomfortable feeling that bad news was about to follow.

"I got that general idea. We're looking for him. But Rae, Dakota didn't check in. I was hoping you'd know where she is."

Her heart sank.

"Fuck," she said out loud, the expletive barely covering the real emotion in her voice.

"I agree. I have Baker on Bedford. BOLO's out. You come back here and..."

"Have you tried her home? Her parents?"

"I have," he said. "No one has seen her."

"That's impossible! She left at the same time I did."

She couldn't believe what she was hearing or saying. Rae remembered every word she'd told Dakota before they parted. Dakota had been well aware of the urgency.

"We went to pick up Bedford, but he wasn't at his house, or at the company. Maybe he followed us. Maybe he was waiting for her."

"Rae, we don't know that for sure yet."

"We need to check the cameras around Bedford's offices. We parked in the lot, and I left first. She was supposed to call you."

She paused for a second, her heart beating painfully loudly.

"I'll meet you at the parking lot there. If her car is still there..."

She didn't need to spell out all the dire possibilities to Mark.

"I have someone checking the hospitals. Nothing so far."

"Okay. I'll see you there."

How could this day have gone from fairly promising to a nightmare in a matter of minutes?

Even given that she'd known her only for a short time, Rae knew in her heart that Dakota would have related the information right away, if she could have.

There was a reason why she hadn't, and Rae was certain that her instincts about Bedford had been right. They had to find him before anything else.

And once they did—she pushed away the thought of why he might have chosen Dakota, given the profile of the other victims. Those questions could wait.

She hoped that Dakota's training would put her at an advantage. And that she'd get to hurt him a little at least.

When she met with Mark in the parking lot, any hope that there might be an alternative explanation was lost. They couldn't find Dakota's car. The two of them traced her and Dakota's steps from where they had arrived, to when they parted in the lot.

Bedford's vehicles were not in this space—he had a private garage here and at home. But according to his staff, no one had seen him here either.

"Why would he go for her? She doesn't fit the profile," Mark said with a frown.

It was almost a relief that he agreed with her on this. Almost, because they had no idea where Dakota was.

"Does it mean anything at this point? She dated his sister. He might have projected some idea of family on her. The Bedfords are close with Dakota's parents. She told me they never interacted much, he might remember it differently. And he feels challenged by her."

"There are cameras around here. She can't just disappear. We will find her."

There was something in Mark's tone that seemed to go beyond reassuring a colleague. If he picked up on how utterly terrified she was at this moment, Rae wouldn't be surprised.

More than that, she was afraid she had fallen for a ruse and lost precious time.

"Let's get that footage," she said.

Chapter 28

U ncomfortable was a mild way to describe her state when she came to, slumped in a chair, her vision still impact- ed. Dakota could only make out shapes in a mirror, herself, someone behind her. The gentle touch to her hair made her shudder, the movement making her more aware of the headache and queasiness.

"You're with us," a soft voice spoke.

The picture was becoming clearer by the second. She was sitting on the chair in front of the mirror, her hands restrained behind her back with zip ties. Part of her wished she could be oblivious a little while longer, because whatever came next, she couldn't imagine it would be good.

The voice belonged to Hannah. That meant she was behind this? Working with her brother all along?

Bit by bit, Dakota's vision cleared, and she could see Hannah standing behind the chair. Tim was leaning against the wall, looking too comfortable for the set-up.

"This is not going to work. You turn yourself in now, you still might have a chance at finding a sympathetic judge, someone who sees all of your story."

Rae would be so much better at this, not that she wanted Rae to be in this situation ever. She couldn't think about this, nor the crime scenes that had brought her to this point. She could barely breathe as it was, and Dakota wasn't sure if it came from getting drugged, or fear catching up to her.

"You can't stop us," Tim said. "We have something important to do."

"Yeah. Murder."

She couldn't keep the sarcasm out of her voice. Dakota's gaze fell on her mirror image, now clear, and she wanted to throw up for real.

She hadn't worn two braids like this since elementary school, and she didn't care for the look now. She hadn't dressed herself in PJs with puppies on them either.

How much time was left?

"You see it your way." Tim shrugged. "I understand that it's painful, but I can promise you, your pain too will end soon. It's what we do, right, Hannah?"

Hannah's expression was unreadable. It was hard to tell if she was scared, apologetic or indifferent.

"And you're okay with this, to be his accomplice, after everything you went through? You lied to us?"

"Yes and no." Tim reached out to brush his hand over one of the braids, making her shudder. The fact that none of the victims had been sexually assaulted was a comfort, but it was a limited one. They had still ended up dead, poisoned.

"It's true that Hannah was my first attempt, but then I realized she was stronger than the others. That I could use her help...and she was ready to give it, weren't you?"

She still didn't react.

"In any case, she needs to leave now," he said. "She has dinner to prepare. You and I have something to talk about."

"Stop it, Tim. If you go through with this, there's no way anyone can help you. Hannah! You know this isn't right."

The woman walked out of the room, ignoring her, and Dakota gave a futile yank at the restraints. The movement made her feel seasick.

"You know what's not right? The way our parents treated us. Stuff like that, it leaves marks. I'm sure you've seen it a lot on the job. Sarah and Marla were better off dead instead of reliving the abuse time and again. I know you can't see it right now, but you too need peace."

"I know what you're trying to do, but you got it wrong. I wasn't abused."

"Maybe it's not something you can admit yet," he suggested. "I had a few conversations with both of them, and finally they realized that it was for the best. You will too."

Dakota hoped that when the time for his trial came people wouldn't be fooled. She was furious. At herself, to some extent, because she could feel fear clouding her mind. Mostly at him, because he thought she was buying the crap he was trying to sell her.

"You thought you were helping." She had to try anyway. "You thought you were protecting Hannah, and the others, but see, they were doing fine. They had lives and jobs."

"So do you, but you aren't happy."

She wasn't going to tell him that she'd been well on her way to happy. She still wanted that chance, so she had to keep him talking while Hannah...Dakota wished the woman could have the presence of mind to call 911, but more likely she was preparing another poisoned meal. Another shudder wound its way down her spine.

"Why do you think that is? You want to put me out of my misery, I think you owe me an explanation, don't you?"

"You're right," he said, his tone now light and conversational as he pulled himself a chair and sat across from her.

Dakota cast a quick glance at the vanity in front of the mirror. The surface was empty, nothing she could have used as a weapon. If she had been able to grab it.

"Look, maybe it's not as severe as in Sarah's case, but I know you were a lonely child. Mona told me your parents neglected you a lot. Maybe that's what happens with rich people and their daughters. For me, my life changed drastically the moment I was adopted. I guess they really wanted a son."

"Good for you."

Wanted it so badly they were willing to help cover up attempted murder? Murders?

"It was. Anyway, they should have taken better care of you. I know about the neighbor, Dakota."

"What neighbor?"

Dakota was starting to believe that not only he was exaggerating, but he had also mixed up her story with that of another woman.

"You don't remember telling Mona? I can't believe that. Where else would she have heard the story?"

"Stop it. There is no story." She took a deep breath, unwilling to fall for his manipulation. She had to gain control. It was the only way she could make it out alive. Out of the corner of her eye she could see the window. The dolls. They were prepared.

"Martin."

She could see his eyes narrow. Tim Bedford didn't like to be reminded of his old life unless it was entirely on his terms.

"That's not my name."

"What happened to the girls in the group home? The ones that were never found?"

He didn't meet her gaze, shaking his head.

"Did Hannah help you with them too? Was it all just an act when she said she didn't want to live under the same roof?"

"She almost got me arrested!" He was nearly trembling with anger and indignation, all of a sudden too close in her face. "Don't make me angry, okay? That never turns out well. Hannah did and look where she is now. She owed me."

"Were you mad at Sarah too? And Marla?"

"They understood in the end. You will too." He patted her cheek, smiling when she shrank away. "I better go check on that dinner."

She wasn't going to accept any food in this house. Better yet, by the time he returned, Dakota planned to be long gone.

Chapter 29

B edford's employee provided the security footage right
away—if it was because he didn't like his boss, or a police
lieutenant was asking, wasn't clear. Rae didn't know or care.

Back at the station, they watched the recording in Mark's
office.

Rae was furious and terrified at the same time. She could see
the disbelief in his expression as well.

The cameras worked perfectly fine. She could see Dakota
leave the building and head for her car, but the footage didn't
extend all the way to her parking spot, so Rae couldn't see her
get in. Something had happened between that moment and
now.

Tim Bedford was still missing but judging by everything she
knew about him and this case, it wasn't much of a stretch to
think he could be this bold.

"Son of a bitch. He must have tampered with it."

"It's possible. We don't have a lot of time," she said. "If he
gets to make one of his fucking dinners, it will be too late."

"Rae. We have every available cop on this. We're going to find them."

"What if it's too late?"

Rae hadn't meant to give herself away, not at this moment of all moments, but she could see realization dawn in his face. He knew that she would want to move heaven and earth for any colleague missing, and yet, this was different.

How ridiculous that they'd even spend a second on worrying about what other people might say, Dakota's parents, Gen...

"Sit for a second, okay?"

"I can't."

"You're not going to help anyone if you keel over."

God, she hated to admit he had a point. Reluctantly, she sat in the visitor's chair.

"Better. Okay, obviously you were getting too close for comfort. You went over his finances. He has properties all over, I assume?"

"Nothing in his name that stood out," she said, feeling despair creeping into her mind. She had dealt with missing persons cases before. Too many didn't have a happy ending. Rae forced herself to think. "He has his condo, and there's the parents' mansion. A few commercial spaces. But he always went to the women's homes."

They had sent someone to Dakota's apartment. It was empty. There was no basement anyway.

"Does Dakota own any property aside from the apartment? Do you know?"

"No, but we'll find out," he promised. "I think it's time you talk to her parents."

Rae wasn't looking forward to it, but she knew she had no choice. She needed to keep moving.

Rae found Mr. Lord at home. He agreed to speak to her, but voiced his opinion clearly after Rae detailed the reason for her visit.

"Tim? This is absolutely insane! Do you know how long we've known this family?"

If she wasn't so single-mindedly focused on one goal, the most important goal, she might have given him a piece of her mind for worrying about his friendship with the Bedfords.

"Mr. Lord, Dakota is missing, and so is Mr. Bedford. It is urgent that we find both of them, so if you have any idea, I need to know now."

He shook his head, apparently still not fully believing her.

"He wouldn't hurt her. He's always been polite to her and my wife. Never heard any complaints from anyone else either. There would have been allegations...No. You must be wrong."

Maybe he was in denial, but Rae wasn't willing to indulge him. Lord must have understood that she was a heartbeat away from yelling at him because he took a half step back.

"If Dakota bought anything else than the apartment she's living in, I don't know about it. And if you must know, we never threatened to disown her for being gay. It's her life. There are a few assets that she will obviously inherit, like the company, this house, and our vacation homes."

Vacation *homes*? In plural?

Rae was sweating. It might be a hot flash, or her patience with Dakota's father coming to a quick end. How could he be so callous about the situation?

"Are any of them within driving distance?"

She felt sick to her stomach at the idea that she might be going at this wrong. But Bedford had killed here, in this city where he and Hannah had lived as children. He wasn't going to fly Dakota out of state? The problem was, technically he could.

They had notified airports in the area in case Bedford was trying to flee.

In that case...

"No, not really...But wait a minute. We have another small apartment building that belonged to my late mother-in-law. It's pretty dated, and there isn't much of an income to be generated from it—"

"Mr. Lord!"

"I might have mentioned it a couple of times when Tim and his parents were present, but I didn't think...All right, here's the address. I don't know what you're hoping to find there, but please, don't break anything. I'm sure Dakota will be fine. She's resourceful."

Rae had more to say, but this wasn't the time. "Thank you. We'll be in touch."

"I hope you'll clear this up as soon as possible."

You and me both.

Walking to her car in brisk steps, Rae took out her phone and called Mark. "I have an address," she told him. "I'm going to check it out right now."

"Rae, hold on a second. We're talking about the guy who already had someone shoot at you, remember? Text me the address and wait for back-up."

"I know procedure," she snapped at him, though she was grateful he didn't mention what else Bedford had likely done. "Just sent it. Why don't you get off the phone and get me that back-up?"

Much to his credit, he chose to ignore her slightly inappropriate communication with a superior.

"You know you'll be crossing county lines, right? I'll make the calls, but when you get there, wait. That's an order in case that wasn't clear. Keep me up to date."

He had hung up on her. She could feel her jaw drop a little, though for one, she didn't have time to dwell, and she had to admit he was right too. She would get to the building, take a careful look around. She would wait for back-up before engaging...

Unless.

Rae pushed the thought from her mind and got into the car. For the next few minutes, she focused on driving, trying hard not to slip into worst-case scenarios. They had been quick. Lord was right in one thing, his daughter was resourceful. Dakota knew they were looking for her, and she would do what she could to stall him.

She would be all right.

It all fit, the family connection, the grandmother's house that undoubtedly had a basement. Rae didn't think Dakota's story was anything like Sarah's or Marla's, but she could read between the lines, something that Bedford might have picked up. Even though her parents had provided her with everything material, Rae sensed a distance in the way they interacted, the way they talked about one another.

It felt...cold. Tim Bedford aka Martin Kinsley might have seen it too, and he'd had a lot more time to observe these dynamics.

No matter what, she was determined to bring Dakota home tonight. She'd show her that someone cared, despite her own family acting appallingly callous.

Chapter 30

Her mind clearer than it had been a few minutes ago, Dakota realized that the place was more familiar than she thought. When her maternal grandmother, the building's original owner, was still alive, she had rented out the place. Sometimes, she had taken Dakota with her when she had business here. Dakota would play with the tenants' children, and when they went home, Grandma reminded her that she would one day own the place, but, after she died unexpectedly, Dakota didn't return.

Her parents had kept it for, in their own words, sentimental reasons, but even relegated to just this room, she could tell that updates were in order.

Apparently, not all the units were rented either.

She leaned forward until her face almost touched the surface of the vanity, suppressing a groan.

Tim's set-up was nothing if not predictable. Her modern apartment didn't have a basement, so he couldn't very well live out his fantasies there. Her grandmother's old-fashioned house with a couple of rental units made a much better crime scene.

Sarcasm was fine. It kept her from panicking, even when Hannah returned to set the table in the corner. For two. Apparently, she wasn't part of the ritual. Dakota wasn't sure how to interpret her gaze. Appalled. Disgusted. With Dakota? Herself?

"If you call 911 right away, they'll be here within minutes. We can end this now, and you can finally move on."

Quiet resigned Hannah was a world away from the swearing woman they'd met on their first visit. The memory was oddly calming—not because Hannah had deceived them both, but because of Rae. The hotel room.

Dakota took a deep breath and got to her feet. She felt a little less dizzy than before. While her wrists were still tied, they hadn't tied her to the chair. Not yet? She wasn't going to wait to find out.

"Stay where you are," Hannah warned.

She held a fork in her hand. Dakota wasn't going to be careless.

"You don't want this. You know how it's going to end."

"As long as it's you, it's not me," the woman returned, and Dakota could see a bit of her more familiar persona return.

"But that's his goal, isn't it? In the end, it will be you, unless you come clean. You can still get away from him. We can help you!"

"We, who?" Hannah laughed bitterly. "The police? Or his father?" She hesitated, then laid down the fork. "You know what he told me when we were down in that basement? Someday, no one will say no to him. Well, Martin was right. He got himself a new name, and a new set of parents, and now everything is possible. He can get to everyone. I'm sorry. It's not personal, Detective."

"It's personal to me."

She made it all the way to the door before Hannah moved. Dakota tried to tear herself out of her grip. She could have overpowered her any day, but with her hands behind her, every move was too awkward, and they both toppled to the floor.

A moment later, the door opened.

"What's going on in here?" Tim sounded amused. He bent down to cut the zip ties while Hannah struggled to her feet. "Now, please, play nice. Dinner's almost ready, and we won't need those anymore." As if reading her mind, he continued. "That's a courtesy. Don't even think about it. There are cameras in this room. I can monitor you on this," he held up his phone, "and I have a gun on me. I'll give you a few more minutes to come to terms with reality. Then we can eat, and you can tell me about the neighbor."

Why did he keep bringing that up? How could he know?

His smile chilled her to her bones. Dakota knew how she needed to use those minutes. If she failed...she wouldn't make it out of here alive.

The moment the siblings had left the room she went to the window. Like in the other killing rooms, it was too high to serve as an escape route. She pulled a chair and picked up one of the dolls, banging it against the window in a futile attempt. A small noise made her stop. Were they back already?

She reached for the handle and barely ducked the next moment when the whole window came out of its hinges and fell to the floor, the glass cracking. For a few heartbeats, she just stared at the mess. This was how her parents had taken care of the place? Perhaps she should take matters into her own hands and pay for those updates. Not the time, she reminded herself.

She pushed the chair aside and went for the table instead. It was heavy, but she managed to drag it across the room to the window. The vertigo came out of nowhere, and she stumbled, but stayed on her feet. Next, she climbed on the table. It still required some acrobatics, but she had made it halfway out the window when she heard the footsteps. *Damn it, no.* She was so close to freedom. Something scraped along her side, and she yelped, but continued to move forward until she collapsed on the lawn. When she got to her feet, Dakota could see that the silly PJs were torn, and warm blood from the cut was staining them.

Something to deal with later.

"Oh, Dakota, I can't believe you are this naïve. I told you, you're not going anywhere."

He had told her he had a gun, but he wasn't holding it now. In fact, his stance was relaxed as he walked closer. If she ran, he might shoot her, unless he had lied about the weapon too. Dakota had to take her chances. Her dash across the yard was more desperate than wild.

"Come on. Time for dinner!"

She had to reach the gate. Beyond it, the real freedom waited. And a lifelong prison sentence for the asshole who had thought of her as prey. Never again.

Chapter 31

Rae knew the moment she laid eyes on the building. The house, its surroundings, everything was too similar. Martin Kinsley always went for a setting that reminded both him and his victims of childhood.

She had no time to lose. She waited until she could hear the sirens and headed around to the back where she assumed the doll window would be.

"Don't be silly," she heard him shout. "You won't make it far. If they're coming for me, you're done too!"

A few heartbeats, and she could see him stumbling across the yard. She advanced closer.

"I will find you," he swore.

"No, you won't, asshole. Put your hands in the air where I can see them."

For a few seconds, everything seemed frozen in time. His face changed expressions several times, from anger to disbelief to the same patronizing smile she was used to from him, Tim Bedford battling back his old self, Martin Kinsley. She could tell that he was about to gauge his chances. Rae trained her weapon on him.

"Hands up!" she yelled.

"Where is your backup, Detective Burton?"

"Right here," Dakota who had appeared behind him, said. She swiftly searched him and produced a gun.

"Fuck you!" He was screaming now. "This is not right. This is not how it's supposed to be! Now you can never be saved!" He struggled, but between the two of them, they wrestled him to the ground, and Rae put the cuffs on him.

Bedford kept yelling and kicking, but Rae didn't care.

"Stop it! You're not helping yourself!"

"Rae, what the hell!"

Castillo had arrived with backup. She couldn't deny that his timing was impeccable.

"I told you to wait," he started, but Rae left Beford to him and the uniformed officers and rushed to Dakota's side.

"Are you hurt?" she asked, aware of her urgent and breathless tone as she carefully checked her for injuries.

Dakota shook her head, but before she could speak, Rae's hand touched the fabric of the PJs appropriate for a child. Her fingers came away wet, and even in the dark she understood what it was.

"You're bleeding!" Louder, she called Mark, "Get us a First Aid kit! She needs to go to a hospital, now!"

"I'm fine," Dakota said quietly, though up close, she was ghostly pale. She swayed a little, and Rae reached out to steady her, glad when the uniformed officers took Bedford away to the squad car. She had a million questions, but one was the most urgent.

"What happened?" Castillo asked after he'd run over to them, bringing the kit with him.

"I cut myself going through the window. That's all. It will be okay."

"Regardless, an ambulance is on the way," he informed them. He patted her shoulder lightly. "Sit down until they arrive, okay? And Rae, we need to—"

She ignored him for a second time and instead directed Dakota to a nearby bench. Eventually, she would have to answer for her actions, but not now.

Dakota leaned into her, her eyes fluttering shut.

"Stay with me, okay?" She touched the fabric again, alarmed at the amount of blood. From the First Aid kit, she retrieved some gauze which she used to apply pressure on the wound. "Please."

"I'm okay. You need to find Hannah. She was in on it, and I think so were Tim's parents. She..." Dakota looked sick to her stomach for a few seconds. "She was making dinner." She didn't pass out, but Rae breathed a sigh of relief when the paramedics finally arrived and took over.

"Will you join me later? At the hospital?" Dakota asked, seeming alarmed all of a sudden.

Ignoring all audience, Rae kissed her temple softly. "Of course."

Two more officers came out with Hannah, one of them informing Rae and Mark that she'd been waiting in the kitchen and did not resist arrest.

Mark insisted on riding with Rae to the hospital, but at least he had postponed the scolding.

"We're going to need her statement. Then you can have a few minutes," he said.

Rae figured it was an appropriate moment for some preemptive explanations.

"I'm sorry," she started, and he made a dismissive gesture.

"Not now. Let's make sure she's okay, and that we have everything to keep him locked up forever. That's all that matters for now."

"I didn't mean to—"

"We can talk about you disobeying my orders later. You don't have to worry about anything else. That's none of my business."

She remained silent after that, deciding to bring up the subject of disclosure with Dakota once she was up to it. Which wouldn't be tonight, and unlikely in the next few days.

"Don't worry. They'll take good care of her."

"I know."

The sky had darkened, rain now pounding against the window. Washing away all confusion. The story was clear to her now.

She was still worried sick.

Dakota looked exhausted, but alert when they could finally see her, and she told them what she knew.

"Maybe I should have stayed and taken my chances down there," she said ruefully. "It was a big risk. I didn't know what Hannah would do."

It would be a long night, but Rae didn't mind. She felt a lot better knowing Dakota was safe and getting the care she needed—wearing a hospital gown instead of those ridiculous PJs. She had undone the braids as well, her hair falling down to her shoulders in messy waves. She looked young, and vulnerable, and Rae couldn't wait until Mark left the room.

"You did well," he said.

"Right. I got the stitches to prove it."

"Let me know when you'll be back at work. I'll wait for you downstairs," he said to Rae. Despite the joke, the relief in his voice was audible. Rae was relieved too, as she turned to Dakota and carefully embraced her.

"I thought he'd never leave," Dakota whispered.

"Same here."

She still had many questions, but Rae wasn't in a hurry to ask them. She just wanted to be here, hold her, assure herself that everything would be okay. That they would be okay.

Dakota held on to her for a few minutes before she let go. Rae could sense her reluctance, mirroring her own.

"I can call Mark and tell him to go. I can catch up with them tomorrow."

"You should go too, before Baker takes all the glory."

It wasn't hard to see past the light tone. Rae had only been with this unit for a short time, but Baker didn't strike her as the type.

"Yeah, well, what if I don't care?"

"You need to finish this," Dakota insisted. "For me, then. I mean it. Go."

"We'll talk later, then. You'll be okay?"

"I got stitched up, and they gave me some good pain meds. I'll be fine. If you could drop by my apartment and get me some clothes tomorrow, I'll be forever grateful."

"I'll do that." Rae reached out to brush her fingers over Dakota's cheek. "And I promise you won't have to wait until tomorrow. I'll figure something out."

"You'll sneak past the nurse?" The hint of a smile appeared in her tired expression.

"I'll sneak past anywhere. I'll be back as soon as I can, clothes, glory, and all. I promise."

Dakota's fingers tightened in the front of her shirt as she pulled her close for a kiss.

"Thank you."

"You're welcome."

I was so scared for you. That, she didn't say out loud. Perhaps it went without saying.

They didn't get to unravel the entire gruesome story that night, but even so, Bedford was enjoying talking.

"You have no idea what it's like," he said, his tone dripping with disdain. "I did what I could to get both of us out of that basement, and the others? I did them a favor. No one wants to live with stories like that."

Keeping a cool façade, Rae pushed her instinctive emotions aside. Angry. Horrified at the idea that they might be finding more bodies.

"So, you decided to end the story for them, whether they wanted it or not."

"Sarah couldn't stop talking about how much she wanted to give other kids opportunities that she never had. Marla was killing herself with her job and studies. Don't you think they have peace now?"

"What about the girls in the group home?" Baker asked. "You wanted to give them peace too?"

Bedford gave him a wide grin. "Yes and no. I was practicing."

Rae wanted to throw up. Before Baker could follow up on his question, she said, "This is all bullshit, and you know it. Your sister could have had a life if you had left her alone. Sarah and Marla had thriving careers, and those girls? They might have had a chance if it wasn't for you."

He fixed her with the same obnoxious grin. "I told you that you wouldn't understand, and so far, nothing you've said could disavow me of that notion. Detective Burton…aren't you going to ask me about Dakota? You were her date at the Lords' dinner. Aren't you curious?"

She could tell from the minute change in his expression that Baker might be curious, and for sure, Mark, who was watching behind the glass got another piece of information he didn't ask for.

"It doesn't matter. That was your biggest mistake, going for a cop. Don't you understand that we have everything we need already? This is a formality."

"I wouldn't be so sure," he said. "Wait until we bring in the experts, and they'll testify to my childhood trauma. Don't you understand that all I wanted was to help them? Even Dakota?"

Rae remembered how he had referred to Dakota's relationship with Mona when they first interviewed him, entirely inappropriate. She assumed this was more of the same, though she felt uneasy about his words. Unfortunately, between him, his parents, and expensive lawyers, someone might try to move the goalpost. It was their job to make sure they wouldn't get far.

"She doesn't need your help."

"Did she tell you about that neighbor?"

"Don't try to distract. It's not going to work." She felt a drop of sweat snake down her back, uncomfortable and worried about Dakota's private life being dissected in this room. It wasn't right. The fear that had gripped her tightly earlier was rushing back, not for something that had happened tonight, but before…

"One time, when they got drunk together, she confided in Mona. Mona told me. That's the story. I don't care that she's a cop. Anyway, picture this gated community, parties with well-dressed people, kids splashing in the pool…Only in one of those houses, the son liked watching those kids change into their bathing suits. Took pictures, even."

Baker cast her a quick glance as if to gauge her reaction.

"Did anything else happen? I don't know, but the worst was that Dakota's parents acted like it never happened. The voyeur's family was quietly shunned by the others, they sent their son away, and that was it. Nothing ever came of it, because no one wanted the attention and the headlines that would have come with reporting him. Sucks when parents don't do their job, doesn't it?"

"You, on the other hand, lucked out with your adoptive parents. They were very supportive." Rae kept her emotion out of her tone. He was getting to her, and the last thing she'd do was let him have the satisfaction of knowing it.

"They sure were."

"Yeah, let's talk about that for a minute."

Chapter 32

Despite her bravado, Dakota regretted sending Rae back to work. She felt much too wired to sleep, but she didn't want to take any medication other than what was already in her system.

The past few hours felt jarringly unreal, but if she really started thinking about it, the past weeks kind of did too, and that scared her a little. Rae would be back with clothes, and her calm and reassuring ways. Rae Burton, her partner. Lover. She might have dreamed it all. She might still be down in that basement with the creepy dolls, about to die...She jerked out of a half-dream, frantically touching the fabric of her gown, assuring herself she wasn't wearing the PJs anymore.

"Hey." Rae stepped into the room, looking as exhausted as Dakota felt, but she was smiling. And carrying a bag hopefully containing a set of clothes. Tomorrow, come what may, she'd sign herself out. The stitches would be an outpatient procedure, normally, but given the fact that she'd been kidnapped by a freaking serial killer, the doctors had insisted on an overnight stay. She had texted her parents that she was okay and would talk to them tomorrow.

They hadn't objected.

"What are you doing here? Shouldn't you go home and feed your cat?"

"Rex is fine. We found your car behind the house, by the way, and your purse was still in it. I brought you something to wear tomorrow, and a pair of your own PJs."

"You're a saint. I'd love to get into them right now."

The eager movement made her wince.

"Easy. Let me help you. You got stitches today."

"So everyone keeps reminding me. Thank you. Again."

She was grateful for Rae's presence, her careful touch, but even so she couldn't shake the surreal feeling.

"How did it go with Bedford?"

"Pretty much as expected."

Did she imagine that hint of caution creeping into Rae's tone?

"More, please."

"He was happy to talk, though he still imagines that some expensive expert might get him off somehow. He might be delusional about that, but he knows what he did. If we hadn't caught him, he would continue to do it."

"Yeah. I got that impression."

Rae was silent for a few heartbeats, worrying her.

"Anything else I should know?"

"No. We got it covered."

"I get it." Dakota sighed. "I don't mind that you get to wrap this up with Baker, but..."

"Don't worry. No one will forget what you put on the line for this case."

She appreciated Rae's wording of the issue—given the fact that after all the work she'd put in, the connections she'd made, she had been kidnapped. By the son of her parents' friends, her ex's brother no less. No wonder she felt off, like none of it was real.

Dressed in her own PJs, with the familiar scent of her laundry detergent, she leaned back against the pillow.

"You should go home," she said, even though it was the last thing she wanted.

"I should let you sleep..." Rae hesitated. "But I could stay a while."

"All right. Thank you."

She had assumed that Rae would sit in the chair, but to her surprise and delight, Rae slipped out of her shoes and carefully lay next to her.

Dakota could finally close her eyes without panicking seconds later. Safe was a relative term at the moment, but tonight this was as close as she would get.

There had been no nightmares. It wasn't that surprising. They always came later. Rae had left in the morning to shower and change. She had promised to be back to drive Dakota home when she was released later. In the light of day, a surprisingly tasty breakfast in front of her, she could tackle some questions she had avoided so far.

Much of yesterday was a blur, but she remembered the point Tim thought he had been making. Given Rae's behavior, he had probably tried the same in the interrogation room.

Most of the time, she tried not to think about it, but disappointment and the sense of betrayal had cut deep at the time. She frowned at her plate, willing herself not to give him, give that incident, too much space.

Too late.

She had confided in Mona once, when they had one of their privileged, rich girl outings, an expensive club, too much champagne, too many revelations afterwards. The fact that Mona had shared her story with Tim was just more proof she'd been right to let her go when she did.

She wondered what Rae thought about it all, but yesterday she didn't have the energy to bring it up. She'd have to at some point.

She would have to find the right moment to have this conversation, among others.

"We could drive by the station if there's something you need to do..."

The stern look Rae gave her spoke volumes. Dakota found it as sexy as she found it frustrating. Given that she didn't have a lot of talking room, she settled for the first.

"I cleared it with Mark. We're going home."

"Okay. But you'll tell me everything—"

"Home to rest."

"It's kind of sexy when you try to boss me around."

Rae smiled, to Dakota's relief a lot more relaxed than the day before. In the light of day, things still felt unreal to Dakota, and she knew the best therapy would be to get back to work as soon as possible, though she wasn't kidding herself. Castillo wouldn't let her come back for at least a few days.

"That has nothing to do with sexy. I'm a mom, remember? Establishing boundaries and all."

"Now you're making it weird."

Fortunately, Rae understood the joke, and they laughed together. It felt good, even if the reminder—again—of her stitches didn't. She'd have no choice but to take it easy for a bit, and she couldn't expect Rae to be around all the time.

"I can see you are feeling better. I'm glad. They gave you breakfast?"

"They did, but since I skipped lunch...you think we could stop for a coffee and something sweet?"

"We could, and then bring it home."

"You are impossible."

Rae didn't comment, but her relaxed stance did wonders keeping Dakota in the moment, even though the temptation to slip into the past or worry about the future, or both, was still strong.

While the buttery pastry and hot coffee, not to mention Rae's continued company, were highly enjoyable, Dakota knew there were other subjects they needed to raise.

"So, tell me about the Bedfords' role in all this. You really think they knew?"

"Right now, all I know is they are pissed," Rae said, thoughtful. "But it was all very quick, the name change, trying to erase all connections to the girls in the group home...I'm not sure, but we're still looking."

"I can't imagine doing that for everyone."

"Perhaps someone, something could have turned him around at that time. Pretending he didn't do the things he did, wasn't a good choice."

"True. I guess we'll see how it goes."

The silence stretched and expanded between them.

"Maybe you should lie down for a bit," Rae suggested. "I'll check on you later?"

"Come on, I'm not tired after all that coffee. You don't have to babysit me either. I guess I'm going to call my parents."

Rae's eyes went wide.

"They haven't called you yet?"

"To be fair, they don't know all the details. We texted yesterday, and I said I was going to call...I guess they still can't believe what he did. Hell, I'm having trouble."

"I imagine," Rae said softly. "I'm sorry."

Her words seemed heavy with meaning, and all of a sudden Dakota couldn't bring herself to wait for a better moment.

"I guess he told you about the other time they didn't do much. Please," she said quickly when the alarm showed on Rae's face. "It wasn't anything like what Marla and Sarah went through. It sucked that no one seemed to take it seriously, but he never touched any of us."

"It was still wrong. And shunning someone from neighborhood gatherings is not the same as holding them accountable."

Dakota took a sip of her coffee, and, realizing it had gone cold, sighed.

"I know. I just...I didn't want you to get the wrong idea."

"Don't worry. And for what it's worth, he pretty much said the same when we asked him why he targeted you."

For a few seconds, she felt her composure slip, tears prickling behind her eyes. Not because of anything she didn't know already. By we, Rae likely meant Baker and Castillo, and by proxy, everyone who would have access to the interrogation tapes and transcripts.

She was familiar with the way victims' lives were analyzed and dissected for the goal of solving a case. She had never been on this side of it. Victim.

215

Rae didn't seem in a hurry to go anywhere, patient to let the moment pass. Dakota drank another sip of her cold coffee, composing herself. She was good at it. She wouldn't give her colleagues any excuse to treat her differently—least of all Rae.

"It's okay. I know you had to. And now you have to get back to work. If they had anything to do with it, they can't get away. These women might still be alive, and...I..." She took a deep breath. "Well, it all comes back to those stitches for me. This could be all nice and smooth," she said, indicating her side.

It was working. For a brief moment, Rae seemed to be distracted. Good to know she was still tempted by what was underneath that shirt—and would be, once those stitches were gone.

"We won't let them get away," Rae promised. Reluctantly, she got to her feet. Dakota saw her to the front door.

"I'll be fine. I promise. I'll watch some TV and read a bit."

"Okay then." Rae pulled her in a close embrace, and all of a sudden, there were many more things Dakota felt she needed to say, like how grateful she had been for Rae staying the night. Had she even mentioned that?

How Rae was right about her parents, hell, even Tim Bedford had a point saying they didn't do the best job back then, not that if justified any of his actions.

The dilemma of feeling alone and needing to be alone was impossible. She wished they were over at Rae's, so she'd have at least Rex to keep her company.

Dakota didn't say any of those things. "You don't have to come over tonight. I'll probably order something and go to bed early."

"We'll see." Rae kissed her softly before she turned and left.

The door falling into the lock, even gently, sounded terribly final.

Chapter 33

Rae had stopped by that night after all, but she didn't stay this time. She sensed that Dakota needed space after a harrowing experience, and she made sure she did everything she could to let her know she would be available.

And then there was work...Specifically wrapping up the case with all its ramifications.

Hannah had made a full confession. Bedford senior claimed that all he had intended was to help a "troubled boy," and that he didn't know about any murders Tim had committed.

They had to let him go.

They had to let it go.

Would it be enough closure for the women's loved ones? For her? For Dakota?

"Good job," Mark said to her when she picked up her coat, about to leave for the weekend.

"Was it?"

The thought of what might have happened to Dakota still kept her up at night. They had put the pieces together, solved the case, but Rae wished they could have gotten to him sooner. Before he remembered something Dakota had told her then girlfriend in private. The thought that she might have been on his radar ever since, chilled Rae.

"Come on. He's never going to get out. Detective Lord will be back next week. It's a win for the good guys."

"I guess."

"Your first case with us. I never doubted I made the right decision."

Had she? Rae couldn't help smiling at the unveiled praise. She hadn't asked for it, but it certainly didn't hurt.

"It was a team effort."

"Sure. You're still as humble as I remember." His expression became more serious when he asked. "You've been seeing Dakota."

Rae cleared her throat.

"How is she really doing?"

So, he wasn't talking about their relationship. Even better.

"She'll be all right," she said. "It's a lot to process."

"No kidding. You have a good night and tell her we look forward to having her back."

"I will," she confirmed, seeing no reason to deny anything at this point. "Before I go...I know I just started here, but if it's at all possible, I'd like to take a couple of weeks next month, or the one after."

"I see no reason why not, but remind me again?"

"Sure. Good night."

There was something to be said about having one's old partner for a boss. It made some things easier.

Once she sat in her car, she took out the phone and sent a text. She was willing to wait as long as she had to, but there was something she wanted to run by Dakota as soon as possible.

If that's all right with you, I could pick you up and we could have dinner at my place? I'll drive you home after if you want to. Rex misses you.

Just Rex? The answer came back within seconds.

No, not just Rex. So?

This time it took almost long enough for her to put the phone away. Finally, she could see that Dakota was typing, and she all but held her breath until the message came.

In that case, I'd love to see you both. You're off work?

Yes, I'm on my way.

Rae assumed that the kissing emoji was a good sign. This was a whole lot more spontaneous than she had imagined. Asking Mark about the time off. Suggesting a dinner without going home first. She took a look at her image in the rearview mirror, deciding it would be okay. She hadn't planned anything for the dinner either, but her last grocery run had only been a couple of days ago, and there was always take-out.

Dakota greeted her at the door, ready to go. Rae felt herself smile, the tension vanishing from her shoulders.

"You look great," she couldn't help saying.

"Thanks. So do you."

"Liar," she said, making her laugh.

"I tell it like it is. But I'm intrigued by your offer. What's on the menu?"

"Anything you want," Rae told her on the way to the car. "There's something I wanted to talk to you about."

She let herself get distracted. There was no hurry to raise the subject. After a week of communicating mostly with texts and video chats, she cherished simply being together, dinner, some TV and conversation.

"I wasn't trying to shut you out," Dakota said, out of the blue, later, when they were about to go to sleep. She had stayed after all, though they had stopped at gentle, careful kisses. After Rae had turned off the light, Rex curled up at the foot of the bed.

"I know. Don't worry about it." Rae turned to her.

"I had a lot to think about. I can't believe Bedford senior will just get off like that."

"Yeah. He was throwing his money around, but at least he didn't know how bad it was."

In the dark, Dakota shook her head. "People with too much money do a lot of harmful things, whether they want to or not."

Rae wasn't sure what to say to that other than that she agreed, so she reached out to lay a hand on her arm.

"You know I really don't care about how much money you have, right?"

"That's right. You took a pay cut to do the job you wanted. I don't think you care that much about money." In the course of the sentence, her tone had gone from light to somber, alarming Rae. It was something she had expected though. Experiences like the one Dakota had just gone through weren't over and done with after a week or two, especially given the past issues it had raised.

"Fuck, no, I didn't want to cry about this, not tonight."

"It's okay. I swear. We'll take it one step at a time."

"You've been so damn patient even when I didn't deserve it."

"Maybe, but you definitely deserve it now. No, come on, that was a bad joke." She reached out, and Dakota went into her embrace willingly. Still tense and frustrated.

"I'm serious. Like you said, you had a lot on your plate. It's bound to catch up. These types of cases tend to do that. You did everything you could. I know it, and Mark knows it."

"It's not that. Well, at least not just that."

She paused but held Rae's gaze.

"I can't be mad at everyone and forget how awful I treated you. My parents, Mona, what they did wasn't great, and I'm not happy that Tim apparently shouted it from the rooftop. But this was your decision, your career, and I made it all about me."

Rae had the suspicion that this was just one of many issues Dakota had been wrestling with lately, though a significant one for her. That meant she had to be honest too.

"I'll admit, I didn't expect your reaction. And yes, it was my decision, but maybe you were a little right too. After the divorce I just wanted to move forward. Forward, at least what it meant to me. I might not have thought it through completely, but I don't regret it either. I am where I want to me."

"Me too," Dakota confirmed, and that was all she needed to know.

The next time Genevieve called, she had apparently read up on American news and gathered a surprising amount of information on the case. Or maybe it wasn't so surprising given the international connections of the Bedfords.

"Hey. I try to keep myself up to date with the news, but wow...congratulations. I guess your first case on the new job was a lot bigger than anyone expected."

"No kidding. And thanks. We have an amazing team." She smiled at Dakota who stood on the other side of the table, holding Rex who yawned, looking comfortable in her arms.

"So, how's it going on your side? How is school?" she asked, and Simon made a face.

"Why do you always ask that, Mom?"

"Don't make me worry. Is everything okay?"

"We're great," Gen said. "He's just a little self-conscious about being at the top of his class."

"Simon, that's awesome! I'm so proud!"

"Does that mean you're coming soon?" he asked, hopeful.

"As a matter of fact, I have something planned."

Over his excited cheering and Gen's smile, Rae said, "And by the way I'd like to introduce you to someone. She's going to come to Paris with me."

"Mom! We already know it's Dakota!"

Dakota finally came over, the cat still with her. Whenever she was home, Rex wouldn't leave her side. Perhaps he could sense that she was still dealing with various issues. Most likely, he was just that enchanted. Rae didn't blame him.

"Hi," she said. "I can't wait to meet you all."

As Rae watched the strands of her life entangle, she couldn't help thinking of Bedford who wanted to buy himself a clean slate, first with the help of his parents, then the money he himself had made. It didn't exist for anyone.

She took Dakota's hand, entwining their fingers, the tender gesture hidden under the table. Rae knew, more than ever, that she stood by her decisions, past and present.

"Don't worry. You will," she promised.

Epilogue

Dakota didn't get nervous easily, or maybe that was something that had changed recently…She was happy, truly happy to be in Paris with Rae, eight days to explore the City of Lights in a way she wouldn't have done on her own, or even before with her family. She was excited, about their time together, about meeting Simon. Rae's ex Gen—she seemed nice.

Rae had done better in every department, exes, parents, but there was no point in thinking about that now.

"Are you okay?" Rae asked, giving her a soft, warm smile, and Dakota knew she meant a lot more than this first in-person introduction. They had arrived early, sitting in the cozy, old-fashioned café where they were about to meet Gen, her girlfriend, and Simon. She took Dakota's hand in hers, and it wasn't until then Dakota realized how cold her own was. This had to go well. It was important to her.

"I'm fine," she said, hoping her own smile would convey the sentiment.

A small sound from the bell above the door announced more customers coming in, and Dakota recognized Genevieve. Rae got to her feet, and the boy with Gen practically flew into Rae's arms. She held him tight for a few seconds, her eyes welling up.

Dakota blinked, too. It wasn't that difficult after all because it wasn't really about her. No one was going to ask about her run-in with a serial killer, and no one questioned her presence. Simon let go of his mother and turned to her.

"Hi, Dakota."

"Hi, Simon. It's so nice to finally meet you in person."

He hesitated for a second or so, then hugged her too.

"Rae, Dakota, you're here! Let's get something to eat, we have a lot of plans today."

Rae's expression was both amused and a bit indulgent, and the look Gen gave her, devoid of any scorn, spoke of a familiar dynamic.

"Yes. They have amazing pastries, Mom."

"I'm glad to hear that. We're mostly here for those."

"Mom!"

Everyone laughed, and Gen introduced her girlfriend Anaïs before they settled around the table.

A server came to take their orders, and Genevieve asked for the *Sélection du Boulanger* and a bottle of champagne for every-one, juice for Simon.

Once everyone had their food and drinks in front of them, they clinked their glasses together.

"To family, new and old," she said, and Dakota couldn't agree more. She was more than excited to be a part of this new, found, family.

The Sapphic Suspense Collection

This curated collection brings together nine distinct voices in sapphic romantic suspense. Each book delivers a complete story of passion and peril, featuring protagonists who navigate both danger and desire. Several entries serve as gateways to forthcoming series, offering readers a first glimpse of worlds their creators will soon expand. From gritty city streets to seaside villages harboring secrets, these tales explore the exhilarating intersection of attraction and jeopardy. Each author introduces characters who've never appeared in their previous works, ensuring fresh terrain for both longtime fans and new readers.

- <u>Baking Ice Cubes</u> – Alexi Venice

- <u>Cash Target</u> – Edale Lane

- <u>Clean Slate</u> – Barbara Winkes

- <u>Find Her Keep Her</u> – Kimberly Amato

- <u>Mai Tais and Murder</u> – KC Luck

- <u>Perfecting the Future</u> – Alysia D. Evans

- <u>Saving Chiara</u> – Anne Hagan

- <u>The Fire and the Warm</u> – Kelli Jae Baeli and Melissa Walker Baeli

- <u>Those We Run From</u> – Fiona Zedde

Acknowledgments

When it comes to reading and writing, suspense with sapphic protagonists has always been my first love. I am grateful to all the fabulous authors who didn't hesitate to join the *Sapphic Suspense* project, and especially Anne Hagan, without whom it would not have become reality.

Thank you all for helping shine a spotlight on this genre!

Dominique, my muse for this story, and all the others.

My readers, who are fearless, even when my mind goes to scarier places.

I couldn't do any of this without you.

About the Author

Barbara Winkes writes sapphic crime drama and Christmas romance. She loves writing characters who get the job done, whether it's stopping a predator or saving cherished traditions—while still making time for love. She lives with her wife in Quebec City.

Website: barbarawinkes.com
Instagram & Threads: @barbarawinkes
BlueSky: @barbarawinkes.bsky.social

Also by Barbara Winkes

Crime Drama & Romantic Suspense

Kelli & Merin romantic suspense duology
  Connected series (sapphic mafia romance)
  Crossing Lines Trilogy (sapphic mafia romance)
  Joanna Mitchell Thriller Trilogy
  Carpenter/Harding (starts with *Indiscretions*,
  ongoing detective series with over 15 titles,
  includes the prequel Introductions)
  Jayce & Emma romantic suspense series

Standalone Books

The Amnesia Project
  Amber Alert
  Secrets

Christmas Romance

Bells Will Be Ringing
  A Girlfriend For Christmas
  Christmas Cupid
  Destination Christmas, Next Stop Love
  The Christmas Memory
  The Wishing Tree
  ...and more!

In Audio

Killer Instinct
  The Amnesia Project